中英對照

近代中國風雲人物詩詞

Poems of Shakers of Modern China
English Translation

江紹倫 選譯

Translated by **Kong Shiu Loon**

商務印書館

中英對照近代中國風雲人物詩詞
Poems of Shakers of Modern China – English Translation

選　　譯：江紹倫
責任編輯：黃家麗
封面設計：涂　慧
出　　版：商務印書館 (香港) 有限公司
　　　　　香港筲箕灣耀興道 3 號東滙廣場 8 樓
　　　　　http://www.commercialpress.com.hk
發　　行：香港聯合書刊物流有限公司
　　　　　香港新界大埔汀麗路 36 號中華商務印刷大廈 3 字樓
印　　刷：中華商務彩色印刷有限公司
　　　　　香港新界大埔汀麗路 36 號中華商務印刷大廈
版　　次：2017 年 9 月第 1 版第 1 次印刷
　　　　　© 2017 商務印書館 (香港) 有限公司
　　　　　ISBN 978 962 07 4551 5
　　　　　Printed in Hong Kong

CONTENTS 目錄

前言 PREFACE

葉劍英 ·· 120
YE JIANGYING

1898-1976
23 周恩來 144
ZHOU ENLAI

1901-1972
24 陳　毅 148
CHEN YI

前言

這是一本詩史書，由近代中國三十位風雲志士詩表國家的屈辱、民族反抗圖強、義士獻身的圖畫，悲憫壯麗。

近代中國由列強用武力打開國門開始。英國強運鴉片毒害中國平民，被林則徐擊敗終止了，卻賠了香港。日本在甲午戰爭中大敗滿清海軍，李鴻章於驚惶中出賣國土，讓日本割據台灣。

三十位詩人都志願愛國，每人有獨特的人格和奮鬥方法，亦各有不同的遭遇。有人革命，有人殺敵，有人教育，有人貢獻文藝或科學，有人做好本份，不論身居何地，亦展現文化修養，做一個受人尊敬的"中國人"，一個驕傲於世的稱號。

詩為心聲，是詩人最直接而坦誠的吐露。它赤裸地表現詩人的靈魂，他對個人和他人、事業和理想、成功和失敗的觀照。詩人用文字、心智和情感做媒介，寫出柔和激昂的詩聲，在虛靜中迴盪，超越時空及人事，把歷史中一時之事傳向永恆。

詩人哲學泰斗陳寅恪有"以詩證史"的說法。說實在的，詩詞流瀉的人情，連歷史亦容納不盡。今天，我們在一本書中細讀近代中國三十位風雲人物的詩詞，可以認清每個人的人格和事業功過，同時看清歷史的過程和真實。

近代中國在迷惑和矛盾中走過一百多年，政治和權力鬥爭此起彼落，風雲不定，陷人民於無邊苦海，時間和生命的浪費計算不盡。

我們的困境由列強的武力侵略所引生，更深層的是文化入侵，由一些中國激進知識份子引入。他們看見西方文化的優越形貌，不見西人好戰的醜惡本性。後者用權勢加罪於人，然後高舉"有理"的口號，殘殺一切異己。

我們今天回顧過去，容易看見近代歷史的這種舉動。1919 年的五四運動推動者，以不成熟的認知做基礎，給中國引入各種主義。他們向青年學生宣揚這些"理想"的形式，用激昂的口號鼓動集體行動，打擊和抹殺傳統文化。於是，人民給分為"進步"與"落後"的兩羣，互相鬥爭。

"新思想"對於好奇的青少年有自然的魅力，而"新"是無規無限的。如是，一切"舊"的東西都必須受到淘汰，包括父母和老師的養育教導。發展到最極端，就是紅衛兵在不止十年的"十年浩劫"中，磨滅了全中國人的本性和尊嚴。如今，史書輕輕地說："那是一場惡夢"。

惡夢有一個特點，當夢者經歷到最激動或可怕的境界之時，就即時醒了，或心有餘悸，或睜眼思想，迎着現實。近來，有人説："睡獅醒了"，積極回望和邁前。

中國人於二十世紀八十年代發現，人類進入一個"資訊時代"，而資訊包括新的和舊的，由無孔不入的信息流衝擊"人的狀況"和"人心"。

中華智慧是多元的，儒家創造了人倫秩序和安身立命的方法，以和為貴，以禮為用，以中庸解除執着，以止於至善完成自我。道家創造了"無為"和"有為"的門路，顯發平等對待世間一切及與萬物同春的精神，維護近代所追求的"可持續發展"，包括一個健康的地球生態和人的安心自在。佛家關切宇宙萬法的空假和真實，引導人們身心安頓，怡然自得。這些智慧是中華文化對人類的常新貢獻，指點生命歸宿。人類於二十一世紀夢寐以求的景況。

值得認識，本書所列的三十位近代風雲人物，多數曾經帶着迷惑和矛盾服務近代中國，向青年鼓吹"不破不立"的運動，自己卻畢生抱住古文和古體詩，即使在最受考驗的生死關頭，亦放聲高歌，留下充實而為數不少的佳作，"以詩證史"的材料。歷史不由口號或炮火塑造，而是千萬人的經驗磚石建砌而成。

我當了六十年教授，主講心理學和社會開發，四十年在加拿大多倫多大學。每當我感到孤寂之時，自然會低吟黃庭堅的"桃李春風一杯酒，江湖夜雨十年燈"，無酒而醉。

在美國，李政道在三十歲的英年時刻，推翻物理學"宇稱守恆"假說，大膽提出"宇稱不守恆"的卓見，於1957年同楊振寧一齊獲得諾貝爾物理獎。

他熱愛讀詩和中華智慧，通過跨學科的修養，形成自率、雋逸、審美、幽懷、風骨和自在的人格氣質，凡事"止於至善"。

他讀屈原的《天問》，反覆吟誦："九天之際，安放安屬？隈隈多有，誰知其數？東西南北，其修孰多？南北順橢，其衍幾何？"，幡然大悟。他想，怎麼在2400年前，詩人竟大膽地提出"地球是扁橢圓球體"的科學假設？他後來查明近代科學家測量地球的大小，赤道半徑為6378km，兩極半徑為6357km，說明地球東西比南北長21km，所以它是一個扁橢圓球體。

李政道教授傾心中國詩詞，當他讀到杜甫的《曲江對酒》，心服了，把該詩的末句捧為座右銘："細推物理須作樂，何用浮名絆此身。"

詩不可譯。不少中外學人都一致公認。中國專家更有認為古詩詞不宜譯為白話文。古詩特有的音調、韻致、意境和味道，都染着詩人的景況、情感和志願，其圖像和色彩都不似今天，所以譯文總會有欠缺。

我同意這些卓見，而且確知譯詩的困難。但是，困難需要克服，不同時代的圖像和色彩亦各有輝煌及貼身意義。況且，二十一世紀是資訊時代，各國人民同住"一個世界"，必須互相溝通。詩是純真綺麗的心靈呼聲，流通了可以促進分享，教人類和諧相處。為此，我建議大家努力譯詩，促進世界和平，人間美好。

試看唐代詩人張九齡 (678-740) 寄愛的名句，"海上生明月，天涯共此時"。誰說不宜譯為英文 (或其他文字)，讓今天的德國人、美國人、俄國人、印度人、日本人一齊分享其中的無限美意？例如英譯的"'The moon floods her brilliance over the ocean face, A moment shared by people in all places'"。

本書部份中英文對照詩詞曾上載於 www.wykontario. org 與讀者分享。我慶幸收到熱誠的回饋，十分鼓舞。不少讀者指出，我的英譯不但有助了解原文，而且使原有意境跳躍在當前意況中，啟發幽思。

本書有多方面的教育用途，簡列如下：
1. 幫助讀者欣賞古詩體裁寫近代人情世事，以及古文的抒情優美。
2. 鼓勵大家用人本精神判認歷史上英雄人物的功過和人格。
3. 為各級學校提供歷史課程和素材，幫助學生認識建國道路和志者的投身貢獻，認識愛國觀念。
4. 提供翻譯課程的新方向，尤其是英譯古詩的新範例。

5. 認識中華文化的價值觀，從而看清中西文化的異同和互動路向。認識中華文化方是普世價值。

本書的寫作和上網，長期蒙受何鎮源校長和陳介眉老師的幫助，提供寶貴意見，特此鳴謝。

江紹倫

於多倫多大學

PREFACE

This is a book of poetic history. It contains poems by thirty shakers of historic events in modern China. Together they depict a picture of shameful defeats, valiant defence attempts, relentless striving to build up a strong nation, and patriotic dedications. Painted with mesmerizing lines, shades and emotional colours across time-space, it is a picture of grand proportion.

Modern China began with the military opening up by Western powers. Britain sent opium in huge quantities to poison the Chinese populace. General Lin Zexu defeated the invading ships, and stopped the inflow. In the end, Hong Kong became a colony for compensation. Japan defeated the Manchu navy in the Sino-Japanese War of 1894. An inept foreign minister Li Hongzhang gave Taiwan to Japan as cession. The curtain of modern Chinese foreign relations thus opened for drama till today.

The thirty poets are all patriots, each in his/her unique character and strife. In time, each met with an end different from others. They revolted, fought the enemy, built schools, or contributed to the arts and sciences. Some simply remained honest, cultured persons to stand as "respected Chinese persons", a proud name recognized around the world.

Poems are human soul expressions. They represent the pure inner voice of a poet, reflecting how he regards himself and others, his activities and aspirations, his successes and failures. Poets use language, intelligence, and feelings to tell their thoughts and deeds, creating gentle and loud poetic songs to reverberate in the cosmos, transcending time, space and human affairs, marking temporary events in eternity.

Philosopher cum poet Chen Yinke offered a concept of "poems substantiate history". As we present in one book the poems of thirty poets who had helped to shape modern China, we anticipate readers to find the contents rich, revealing and meaningful. Our readers will see from the words of the poets a clear view of who is what, and identify wise decisions from selfish mistakes. They will then understand history in human dynamic terms.

Modern China had gone through more than a century of confusion and contradiction, filled with ideological and power struggles. In the rise and fall of winds and clouds, our people had suffered difficulties and pains, wasting time and life the loss of which challenged any measurement.

China's difficulties arose from the military invasion of Western powers. But, the deeper spoils emerged from cultural invasion, brought in by our own light-headed intellectuals. They admired the outward superiority of the Western culture, and missed the warring nature of the Westerners. The latter exercises power and authority to cap sin onto people with different beliefs, then vindicates, even kills them "legitimately" based on the alleged sins.

Today, as we review past events, it is evident how we had

fallen into our own traps. In the May-Fourth Movement of 1919, the leaders introduced a variety of ideologies into China separately, based on an immature understanding of each of them. They regarded them as "nation-saving" ideals, and infused them into our youths. They stirred up collective actions to implement those ideals throughout the motherland. In time, our people were divided into two camps, named "progressive" and "backward" respectively, and charged to engage one another into relentless struggles.

That was a major mistake. It helped to create a succession of social-cultural calamities, culminating a "decade of violence" of the Cultural Revolution. They reduced the dignity of the entire Chinese populace to the very base.

Most of the poets in this book are leaders of the "new cultural movement". In life as in thoughts, however, they express themselves with the writing of classical poems, which they do well. Today, as we read the many poems written by these social shapers reflecting their deeds and wills, we can see the poets in clearer perspective, and give them their rightful places in history.

The charm and power of Chinese poetry is evident, flowing through three thousand years. The 1957 Physics Nobel Laureate Tsung-Dao Lee loves classical poems. He read Qu Yuan's Inquiries of Cosmos: "In the space of nine heavens, what rests what belonged? What have and how many, who knows the number? East south west north, which side measures more? South north appears in oval form, what measures to search?" He suddenly wondered how a poet of 2400 years ago could contemplate the shape of mother-earth. The mind of the poet is simply spacious. Later, he looked to find that modern cosmic scientists did make exact measurements to prove that the earth is an oval sphere.

Even physics had been a part of ancient Chinese poetry, to pertain life and human striving. From the lines of Du Fu of Tang Dynasty "One must enjoy the spirit in fathoming physics, and search not for superficial fame to imprison life", Professor Lee found his personal dictum.

Poems do not lend themselves to translation into a different language. Some experts even say that classical Chinese poems should not be translated into modern Chinese. I agree and I know the difficulties of rendition. However, we now live in an Age of Communication and a "one-world" reality. Understanding among human beings of all linguistic and cultural traditions is essential to peace, well-being and survival. We therefore need rendition, the more the better.

Modern technology facilitates the flow of data. Only the presentation of meanings in receptive forms can move people to appreciation, sharing and collaborations, furthering togetherness, respect and universal harmony.

Beauty sharing can nurture the human spirit, propelling it to heights of satisfaction and serenity. Who would not be moved by the Tang poem of Zhang Jiuling: "The moon floods her brilliance over the ocean face, A moment shared by people in all places"? How wonderful it is to feel that one is in Nature's embrace, and the same feeling of security and love is shared with lovers far away.

In the past couple of years, I had the help of Mr. Anthony Ho in uploading some of the poems in this book onto www. wykontario.org for world-wide sharing. Many readers had sent me valuable feedback and encouragement. Many say the English rendition not only helps them to understand the original Chinese poems better, the translated text in modern English shines with relevant meanings in today's bustling life.

This book has many uses because of its rich contents and bilingual presentation.

First of all, it is a book of poetic history of modern China written by a diversity of leaders who had helped to shape it. The materials can be used to write history textbooks for schools.

Second, classical Chinese poems should have a new place in schools as in life. Appearing in different modern languages, profound wisdom, unlimited imagination, linguistic beauties, and spiritual craves, as presented in new renditions, are nourishing food for thought.

Third, translation studies, in theory and practice, can now go forward, with renewing purposes that poems can and must be translated into different languages.

Finally, I believe a true understanding of our recent history will be a powerful motivation for us to learn from our formidable traditions. It should help all of us to regain the confidence that our ancient wisdom constituted the Universal Truths.

I must thank Gertrude Chan and Anthony Ho for the many valuable suggestions in editing.

Kong Shiu Loon
University of Toronto

中英對照近代中國風雲人物詩詞

POEMS OF SHAKERS OF MODERN CHINA –
ENGLISH TRANSLATION

1-30

1

1785-1850
林則徐
LIN ZEXU

Tune: Tall Sun Terrace–Rhyme with Xie Yun My Senior

高陽台：
和嶰筠前輩韻

Jade opium a hefty harvest	玉粟收餘
Golden tobacco leaf they cultivate	金絲種後
British ships bring in smoking evils	蕃行別有蠻煙
Lying down with a double smoking gun at ease	雙管橫陳
Who would not fall into sleeping peace	何人對擁無眠
One knows not enticing tastes lead to addiction	不知呼吸成滋味
Lighting a fire happy	愛挑燈
The night eternity	夜永如年
Most pitiful	最堪憐
A tiny opium ball	是一丸泥
Costs coin strings ten thousand	捐萬緡錢
A spring thunder shatters concaves in Lingding Ocean	春雷欻破零丁穴
To turn frolic mirage into true perception	笑蜃樓氣盡
Power trades deadly terminate	無復灰然
On high grounds at Sandy Cape near Tiger Gate	沙角台高
Fleeing ships hurry toward the horizon	亂帆收向天邊
Whence the Jade Staff joins the Legend Pole	浮槎漫許陪霓節
Behold the glimmering froths	看澄波
Like reflective mirrors in perfect focus	似鏡長圓
It is time to change	更應傳
Back toward the enervate islands	絕島重洋
Ships flurry in new altered directions	取次回舷

Tug Ropes

Climbing a hill is like rowing an up-current boat
One is not free without pulls unlike walking on flat roads
A silky cut in the fog opens a path tiny
Lengthy strings send us into a world of scenic beauty
They say I'm bound for Sichuan to fight with bow and arrow
Or to reach the home of Love Stars using the legend pole
If not tested by the straight measures of justice
Dare I aspire to mount a thousand zeniths to be free

輿纖

山行也學上灘舟
牽挽因人不自由
一線劃開雲徑曉
千尋曳入洞天秋
漫疑負弩經巴蜀
便當浮槎到女牛
不為絲繩標正直
此身誰致萬峯頭

2

1823-1901

李鴻章

LI HONGZHANG

From the Pond

池上篇

In ten acres a house I dwell	十畝之宅
A garden occupies half the dell	五畝之園
A pond water beaming	有水一池
A thousand bamboos surrounding	有竹千竿
It is not a place too small	勿謂土狹
Not away from a port of call	勿謂地偏
Suffice for me to sit	足以容膝
Suffice to quell my worry wisp	足以息肩
With a hall and a yard to stroll	有堂有庭
With a bridge and a boat to row	有橋有船
Books and wines	有書有酒
Songs and strings	有歌有弦
An old man sits in peace	有叟在中
His white beard flows at ease	白須飄然
He knows himself and satisfaction	識分知足
And cares little about other nations	外無求焉
Like a bird roosting in a chosen secure tree	如鳥擇木　姑務巢安
Like a hare in its hole caring not the wide sea	如龜居坎　不知海寬
With a garden of spirited rock cranes	靈鶴怪石
A pond nurturing nuts and white lilies	紫菱白蓮
These my likings	皆吾所好
All in my presence	盡在吾前
Now I take a drink	時飲一杯
Now I write to sing	或吟一篇
My wife and family in harmony	妻孥熙熙
My dogs and hens living happily	雞犬閒閒
Ah leisure and serendipity	優哉遊哉
I shall grow old here heavenly	吾將終老乎其間

（李鴻章引述白居易池上篇）

In the Capital (One of Ten)

I stand a man in hand a long hook my feat
With a will high as a tower of one hundred feet
Ten thousand years of history who will write
Three thousand miles away who be knights
I shall follow the way-side steed in haste
And wait not a minute watching gulls play
On the Lugou Bridge I laugh with the moon nigh
How many people reached the Fairy-land they tried

入都（其一）

丈夫隻手把吳鈎
意氣高於百尺樓
一萬年來誰著史
三千里外欲封侯
定將捷足隨途驥
那有閒情逐水鷗
笑指瀘溝橋畔月
幾人從此到瀛洲

Moonless Mid-Autumn Festival Night

Your pristine lights shine on China since old

Today mist and fog cover your palace whole

Do not let your shadows dim our motherland bit by bit

Dividing our hills and rills their parts no longer fit

中秋夜無月

亘古清光徹九州

只今煙霧鎖瓊樓

莫秋遮斷山河影

照出山河影更愁

Sixteen Poems on River Qian
(V)

On White Crane Tower windows open to four sides
At its foot flows a pristine stream far and wide
Fields around all grow lotus so green
Breezes travel ten miles carrying fragrance clean

潛江雜詩十六首
（五）

白鶴樓中四面窗
白鶴樓下清溪長
田田盡種青荷葉
十里風來併是香

Visiting Hong Kong

到香港

Ocean and sun are from dynasties ancient

Clothing styles are of Han tradition

Watching from the tower all lands are our own

I see no yellow dragon on the flags flown

水是堯時日夏時

衣冠又是漢官儀

登樓四望真吾土

不見黃龍上大旗

Getting Up at Night

夜起

The iron-horse wind chime a thousand times ring

The assault of Eight Western Powers halted for the time being

As we yearn to enjoy peace and security all over

Russia invades our north-east arousing fear

Gloomy stay remains day after day

Under a dim moon how many people stay sane

In the confines of my small study I stand alone to cogitate

Ten thousand families in dreams could pundits keep awake

千聲簷鐵百淋鈴

雨橫風狂暫一停

正望雞鳴天下白

又驚鵝擊海東青

沉陰噎噎何多日

殘月暉暉尚幾星

斗室蒼茫吾獨立

萬家酣睡幾人醒

Two 1899 Poems

Amid time and space changes we migrated
More than a thousand years in the south we had stayed
Our dialect has the same lingual tones of the central plain
As generations before our decorum remains same

The rising eastern sun meets the sea in roaring waves
Human belief in equality for all is again kept awake
This ideal will be in common practice twenty years hence
My prediction is contained in a note hidden deep in a den

己亥雜詩二首

篳路桃弧輾轉遷
南來遠過一千年
方言足證中原韻
禮俗猶留三代前

滔滔海水日趨東
萬法從新要大同
後二十年言定驗
手書心史井函中

Spring Sorrow

春愁

Spring sorrow lingers I look up the mountain

Past events frightful tears ready to fountain

Four million countrymen cry in unison

*A year ago this day Taiwan was in cessation

春愁難遣強看山

往事驚心淚欲潸

四百萬人同一哭

*去年今日割台灣

*17 April 1895

*1895 年 4 月 17 日

Leaving Taiwan

*The Prime Minister has the power to make gifts in cessation

Patriotic legions helpless in reversing the traitorous decision

On a leafy skiff toward drunken land I am sailing

I look back to my motherland feeling sad and unavailing

*Li Hongzhang, 1823-1901

離台詩

*宰相有權能割地

孤臣無力可回天

扁舟去作鴟夷子

回首河山意黯然

*指李鴻章，1823-1901

A Moonless Lantern Festival 元夕無月

For three years the moon emits no light on Lantern Fest Eve　三年此夕月無光
It chooses to shine where our homes used to be　明月多應在故鄉
To catch the moon in sky above the wide sea　欲向海天尋月去
Fly pass the Taiwan Strait in a predawn dream you will see　五更飛夢渡鯤洋

Mountain Village (3 verses)

Amid the clicking sound of the irrigation machine the pool is filled
To this scenic place of hills and rills I hurriedly pursue
Smokes from cooking stoves dance in the forest
Telling everyone dinners are ready at their best

The setting sun shines on a corner of the west mount
Over the east hills clouds break rains falling down
Before the maples turn yellow and red persimmons ripe
Deep in ten thousand mountains autumn is in radiant dye

With a final rain the terrace rice fields are ready for harvest
Their lofty beauty adds charm to this picturesque August
Whence the collecting officers come holding tax bills high
Dogs and hens take flight to alert farmers of their plights

山村即目（三首）

軋軋車聲水滿陂	一角西峯夕照中	山田一雨稻初蘇
溪山佳處客行遲	斷雲東嶺雨濛濛	村景宜添七月圖
林腰一抹炊煙淡	林楓欲老柿將熟	雞犬驚喧官牒下
知是人家飯熟時	秋在萬山深處紅	農忙時節隸催租

Hills of Teas Seen from My Boat

舟中望茶盤山

On a gloomy sea of haze the red sun sets on the horizon
滄波無際夕陽紅

A tall cliff on a lonely islet sits in the middle of the ocean
孤嶼蒼茫大海中

Where the clouds rest the scene appears like ink painting
水墨痕濃雲腳矮

On the hills decorated by rows of tea plants it is mistily raining
茶盤山外雨濛濛

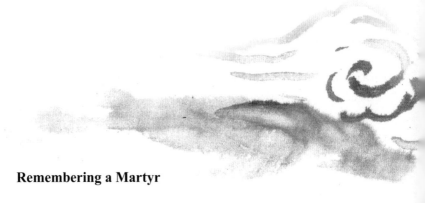

Remembering a Martyr

Half of China south east stood three countries since ancient
Your death leaves a vacuum in our revolution intentions
What is left to do is difficult to say the least
Who could match your leadership in this task mighty
The frontier is full of enemies readying to invade
Our land has a sunset government and people are in sway
Whence we have this inept government overthrown
We will enshrine your deeds with wine wherever rivers flow

輓劉道一

半壁東南三楚雄
劉郎死去霸圖空
尚餘遺孽艱難甚
誰與斯人慷慨同
塞上秋風悲戰馬
神州落日泣哀鴻
幾時痛飲黃龍酒
橫攬江流一奠公

Tune: Prelude to Water Melody–1895

A pair of national gems shattered

How very generous

A song made up by tears and bleeding

No sign of grieving

Three hundred years of imperial comforts

Hills and rills in same old consort

Why change the governing set up

Hundreds of nobles in hard drinking

All four frontiers in fighting

Swords in gold

Lengthy plans on hold

They are but shows

When drunken one engages in rambling

When awake drown in heavy raining

Care not time and life energy gone

Fear youthful thoughts and acts revolutionary

Half exerted void of productivity

I accede to bear the ills of our people

水調歌頭 · 甲午

拍碎雙玉斗

慷慨一何多

滿腔都是血淚

無處著悲歌

三百年來王氣

滿目山河依舊

人事竟如何

百戶尚牛酒

四塞已干戈

千金劍

萬言策

兩蹉跎

醉中呵壁自語

醒後一滂沱

不恨年華去也

只恐少年心事

強半為銷磨

願替眾生病

稽首禮維摩

Self-exhortation (2 verses)
(I)

I have always disliked words babbling
Bustling moans would find no willing recipient
Ten thousand misfortunes arise from ready dependency
A hundred years of diligence prevails with destiny
Self-actualization will further opportunities plenty
Caring for the motherland must never be tardy
Learning to know The Way should precede heroic wishes
I am content to ground my effulgence with peer successes

(II)

Dedicating to improve society I fear not ten thousand darts
Writing to awaken my people I aim to win generations' hearts
I vow to remove obsolete habits to celebrate civil liberty
And organize reasons and wisdom to enrich new knowledge
Ten years hence my deeds should be put in review
Among a boisterous people what will be the burning issues
Our wishes are unlimited in a world of infinite possibilities
To the vast expanse of sky and sea I stand in tranquility

自勵（二首）
（一）

平生最惡牢騷語
作態呻吟苦恨誰
萬事禍為福所倚
百年力與命相持
立身豈患無餘地
報國惟憂或後時
未學英雄先學道
肯將榮瘁校羣兒

（二）

獻身甘作萬矢的
著論求為百世師
誓起民權移舊俗
更研哲理牖新知
十年以後當思我
舉國猶狂欲語誰
世界無窮願無盡
海天寥廓立多時

Spring Thoughts

Admiring spring blooms with warm wine time continues
How quickly a year is gone we meet for friendship renewal
Pity to see war flames west of the river raging ample
Sadly I listen to the toll from the Hanshan Temple

春感

載酒看花興未慵
韶光又是隔年逢
只憐烽火連江右
愁聽寒山寺裏鐘

To Yang Yunshi

We touch palms to exchange views on who are heroes
And cook plum wine to remember our times in the Capital
We left the Pass to pursue flower blooms away from the frontier
And leave poems all over the north-east for people to admire

贈楊雲史

與君抵掌論英雄
煮酒青梅憶洛中
雪裏出關花入塞
至今詩句滿遼東

Sing to Thirty-nine Years

At thirty-nine I ought to know not to err next year
Better return to Nature and keep memories of yesteryear
Most astonishing accomplishments trickle away
I love to appreciate my garden and trees in sunset rays
All worldly business ceases to work in the night
Even monkeys and cranes rest in familiar sites
I stand serene my feelings flow free
Vernal breezes caress my coat as they please

自詠三十九歲

三九年知四十非
大風歌罷不如歸
驚人事業隨流水
愛我園林想落暉
入夜魚龍都寂寂
故山猿鶴正依依
茫茫獨立無端感
時有春風振我衣

Thoughts–Written in Japan

In gloom neither sun nor moon sheds any light
A woman's world is in deep water with no help in sight
I sold my jewellery to go overseas to see the world
And left my children at home east I go
Unbinding my feet I rid off years of poisons in tradition
With a burning heart I stir up women's spirit in motion
Behold this kerchief delicate as it appears
Half soaked with blood half with tears

有懷 —— 遊日本時作

日月無光天地昏
沉沉女界有誰援
釵環典質浮滄海
骨肉分離出玉門
放足湔除千載毒
熱心喚起百花魂
可憐一幅鮫綃帕
半是血痕半淚痕

Written on Board at Yellow Sea to a Japanese Friend Who Show Me a Map of Japan-Russian War on Chinese Soil

Ten thousand miles to and return I ride the wind
Travelling alone to the East Sea thundering in spring
So sad to see the Chinese map in changed colour markings
What government would allow its land reduced to war ashes
This cheap wine drowns not tears grieving for my homeland
To be helpful we must unite many more able and devoted men
I vow to brave my head with hundred thousand others sparing no blood
To turn around the ill fate of our motherland we must resolutely act

黃海舟中日人索句
並見日俄戰爭地圖

萬里乘風去復來
隻身東海挾春雷
忍看圖畫移顏色
肯使江山付劫灰
濁酒不銷憂國淚
救時應仗出羣才
拼將十萬頭顱血
須把乾坤力挽回

Reply to a Japanese Friend

They say in tradition no woman could be a hero
For one thousand leagues on winds I alone rode
My poetic thoughts extend I sail the sky and the sea
In my dreams your island country is beautiful and free
I grieve to note my traditional country has changed hands
Ashamed to know I've not done enough to prevent
My heart bleeds with so much remiss and hate to apprehend
How could I enjoy a peace of mind to be a guest in your land

日人石井君索和即用原韻

漫雲女子不英雄
萬里乘風獨向東
詩思一帆海空闊
夢魂三島月玲瓏
銅駝已陷悲回首
汗馬終慚未有功
如許傷心家國恨
那堪客裏度春風

Thoughts in Prison (1922)

Winds and thunder may blunder over the Pearl any day
The tide to counter the revolution rise and prevail
The musical notes in disharmony the strings in acrimony
To live or die is no longer my worry
Those who know not their identity surrender to destiny
Weeds grown in barren land claim their lives a mystery
We may not measure deeds on a dimensional scale
The country's future is ruined by a termite siege

壬戌六月禁錮中聞變（1922）

珠江日夕起風雷
已倒狂瀾孰挽回
徵羽不調弦亦怨
死生能一我無哀
鼠肝蟲臂惟天命
馬勃牛溲稱異才
物論未應衡大小
棟樑終為蠹蟻摧

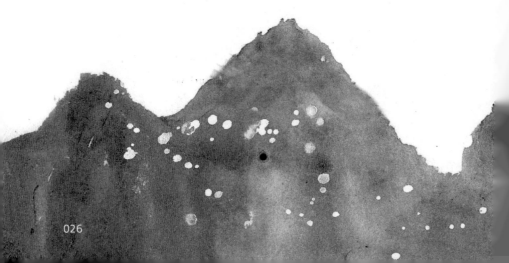

To My Wife in My Imprisonment
(I)

When I am gone your responsibility is imminent
I am confident you will not be less than a heroin
My spirit will remain alive even when body is no more
It will continue to fight mightier than a butcher's knife

(II)

To live is not an envy death not dreary
The universe revolves creating many an opportunity
Forty-five years of worldly toil is a bitter affair
This liberty in death would resolve any wrongs I might fair

留訣內子
（一）

後事憑君獨任勞
莫教辜負女中豪
我身雖去靈明在
勝似屠門握殺刀

（二）

生無足羨死奚悲
宇宙循環活殺機
四十五年塵劫苦
好從解脫悟前非

The Tomb of Qiu Jin

Was assassin of the Qing Emperor an accomplishment
Our present society is still full of uncertain elements
How I like to honour you at the Wind and Rain Pavilion
I lament even though the time is not so

秋女俠墓

見說椎秦願已酬
那知滄海尚橫流
我來風雨亭邊過
不是愁時也欲愁

Weeping for a Martyred Friend

We are not mere acquaintances and school partners
We understand each other doing difficult tasks
Leaving the frontier for home in autumn we felt sad
Before parting we held hands planning to connect
Who is responsible for confusing thieves and master
We believe your death a signal revolutionary matter
Using sad words to register our grief will not do you justice
Recording your good deeds is better than singing a praise

哭執信

豈徒風誼兼師友
尾共娘危識性情
關塞歸魂秋黯淡
河梁揾手語分明
盜猶憎主誰之過
人盡思君死大輕
衷語追華終不是
鈣金牢得似早生

13

1881-1936

魯　迅

LU XUN

Two Untitled Poems

(I)

The Great Yangtze flows east day and night

Daring youngsters gather to go abroad for insight

The spirit of the Sixth Dynasty alive not in dreams

O'er this Rock City the crescent moon shines not dim

(II)

Revolting braves are buried at Yu Hua Tai

On Mochou Lake the revolution spirit thrives

Heroes I admire are seen no more

I sing loud to remember them all

無題二首

（一）

大江日夜向東流

聚義羣雄又遠遊

六代綺羅成舊夢

石頭城上月如鈎

（二）

雨花台邊埋斷戟

莫愁湖裏餘微波

所思美人不可見

歸憶江天發浩歌

The Xiang Spirit

The Xiang River was once pure green
Now blood stained its water is red cream
The Xiang Spirit solemnly gazes at her flow
The pristine waters reflect pink in a moon full
Isolate terrors loom in the dead of night
Fragrant flowers wither spring is not in sight
Drum beats and lute tunes their music never hold
In autumn the west gate's peace images are only for show

湘靈歌

昔聞湘水碧如染
今聞湘水胭脂痕
湘靈妝成照湘水
皎如皓月窺彤雲
高丘寂寞竦中夜
芳荃零落無餘春
鼓完瑤瑟人不聞
太平成象盈秋門

No Title (Enemy swords dance furiously on our noble land)

Enemy swords dance furiously on our noble land

Dark clouds of war loom with no hint of end

Here in my homeland vernal breezes are for the minority

Sufferings and restrictions reign over the majority

Alas my people are content in dreams of past glory

In today's mainstreams joyful songs only in memory

With the unlimited persecution of free expressions

Social conscience and narration of free will are in desolation

無題（大野多鈎棘）

大野多鈎棘

長天列戰雲

幾家春裊裊

萬籟靜愔愔

下土惟秦醉

中流輟越吟

風波一浩蕩

花樹已蕭森

No Title (Spending spring amid long nights of fear)

Spending spring amid long nights of fear
I take refuge with wife and son grey hairs appear
In dreams I see dimly my mother in tears
On the city gate a new flag daily appears
How tormenting that my peers die front and behind
In wrath I seek out meek verses amid sword shines
I chant lowering my brow finding nowhere to speak my mind
Whence my grey coat is showered by cool moonshine

無題（慣於長夜過春時）

慣於長夜過春時
挈婦將雛鬢有絲
夢裏依稀慈母淚
城頭變幻大王旗
忍看朋輩成新鬼
怒向刀叢覓小詩
吟罷低眉無寫處
月光如水照緇衣

Reply to a Friend in Irony

Apathetic men may not be true heroes
Affection for one's young are many so natural
Observe the fierce tigers who frightened everyone with windy roars
They cast loving glances at their cubs as they go forth

答客誚

無情未必真豪傑
憐子如何不丈夫
知否興風狂嘯者
回眸時看小於菟

Seeing Wataru Masuda Home to Japan

Autumn tints are splendid in old Fusang
Bright red maple leaves bring gentle cold along
I break a willow twig to bid you farewell
My heart sails with you to recall my youthful days happy and well

送增田涉君歸國

扶桑正是秋光好
楓葉如丹照嫩寒
卻折垂楊送歸客
心隨東棹憶華年

Impromptu Verses

Poems and prose have the worth of dust what could I do
I raised my head to look east dreaming of culture rich and full
Where scented woods and fragrant flowers are a rarity
Spring orchids and autumn blooms appear separately

偶成

文章如土欲何之
翹首東雲蔥夢思
所恨芳林賽落甚
春蘭秋菊不同時

Written after the 1932.01.28 Battle

War clouds clear in a dwindling spring
Heavy gun-fires and spirited songs in silence sing
I have no poem for our soldiers coming home
From the depth of my heart I wish them ever safe at home

一・二八戰後作（1932.01.28）

戰雲暫斂殘春在
重砲清歌兩寂然
我亦無詩送歸棹
但從心底祝平安

13
1881-1936

魯 迅

LU XUN

Untitled (1933)

The Xiang Spirit rests on a flower specially chosen
Sweet breezes carry orchid scents to comfort the awakened
Unwanted weeds thrive to fill the open plain so wild
Banished orchids will spread the fragrance even in exile

無題（1933）

一支清采妥湘靈
九畹貞風慰獨醒
無奈終輸蕭艾密
卻成遷客播芳馨

Untitled (1934)

Amid the brambles ten thousand gloomy faces hide
Their sorrow songs shatter the earth day and night
Bound to my homeland's conditions my mind finds no rest
In silence I hear shattering thunder arrests

無題（1934）

萬家墨面沒蒿萊
敢有歌吟動地哀
心事浩茫連廣宇
於無聲處聽驚雷

Inscription on My Photo

My heart has no escape but to care like darting arrows
While my homeland is hit by rocks of stormy sorrows
I speak to stars on high they don't seem to care
I resolve to save my motherland with blood I dare

自題小像

靈台無計逃神矢
風雨如磐闇故園
寄意寒星荃不察
我以我血薦軒轅

Hazy Dawn

曉煙

Loaming over brown shrubs maple reds shine

桷葉深黃楓葉紅

Verdant greens in old pines dye up the sky

老松奇翠欲拏空

At dawn there is an air of mystery

朝來別有空濛意

Heavy mist veiled my vast country

都在蒼煙萬頃中

The rising sun mimics the moon to tease the cool sphere

初陽如月逗輕寒

The tree-lined plain seen from a distance is whole and near

咫尺林原成遠看

Remember the beauty of the south under misty rains

記得江南煙雨裏

Maidens stay down river to wash their hair-buns in spring

小姑鬟影落春瀾

Thoughts

Sorrows felt like illness lingering on
Reading history brings tears finding no song
Mellon vines tangle with no harvest possible
To cook peas on peapod fire is so unreasonable
Foreign pipes singing the cool moon ring up no beauty
The river-side town in painting appears in self-pity
Do not turn to view the Capital from afar
Veiled in cold mist random tortures persist ajar

有感

憂來如病亦綿綿
一讀黃書一泫然
瓜蔓已都無可摘
豆箕何苦更相煎
笳中霜月淒無色
畫裏江城黯自憐
莫向燕台回首望
荊榛零落帶寒煙

Composed in My Dream   夢中作

Arriving at Deserted Island	揭來荒島上
Seeing the Illuminouse Horizon	極目海天明
My heart follows the lone sail far	心與孤帆遠
My body light as a paddle bar	身如一棹輕
As froths dance in sunny shadows	浪花分日影
Protruded rocks sing songs of riddles	石筍咽湍聲
Where the broad hazy plain meets the sky	漠漠平煙外
A white crane flies across the sphere leisurely by	翛然白鷺橫

Crimson Leaves

Shying prominence we choose to appear in modesty
Together we drink until tipsy in good company
We recall in late spring the legendary Peach Valley
Where peach flowers tint homes even in remote territories
The sun has left the banks of River Wuding
Willow branches dance freely stirred by the west wind
Crimson not the colour usually seen of the maple kind
They emerge from cuckoo cries marking human sacrifice

紅葉

不成絢爛只蕭疏
攜酒相看醉欲扶
得似武陵三月暮
桃花紅到野人廬
無定河邊日已昏
西風刀翦更銷魂
丹楓不是尋常色
半是啼痕半血痕

14

1883-1944

汪精衛

WANG JINGWEI

Sitting in the Rain

Distant trees on this vast plain appear floating in the sky
Their leaves rustle singing songs divine
I ponder where to rest this imperceptible grief
West winds blow rains fall to veil everything in mist

坐雨

荒原遠樹欲浮天
黃葉聲中意渺然
為問閒愁何處去
西風吹雨已如煙

In Poet Deng's Rhyme

Spring hills beyond the woods seen and unseen
Icy pond waters dripped to overflow so keen
Where behind fences people sang off and on
Red plum blooms filled a tree their brilliance shone

鄧尉山探梅口占

林外春山斷復延
泮冰池水乍涓涓
人家籬落歌疏處
一樹紅梅分外妍

Self-deride–1944

Nothing matters as darkness dims my inner world
Complaints reign throughout our motherland evermore
Our fore-runners bore heat and cold for change in vehement zest
Will new generations continue their historic cause I dare not guess

自嘲 —— 1944 年於病榻

心宇將滅萬事休
天涯無處不怨尤
縱有先輩嘗炎涼
諒無後人續春秋

Imprisoned–1910

Loudly I sing in my ancient home town
Mind at ease I don on this prison gown
To the executioner's swift sharp knife
My youthful head extends my life in strife

被逮口占 —— 1910

慷慨歌燕市
從容作楚囚
引刀成一快
不負少年頭

Ascending Mount Yuelu (1905)

Verdant blue cloud-tall trees spear the sky
Ten thousand hills and rills appear in sight
I survey the central plain wondering who the ruler be
To the peak I quietly ride on my steed

登嶽麓山（1905）

蒼蒼雲樹直參天
萬水千山拜眼前
環顧中原誰是主
從容騎馬上峯巔

16

1884-1918
蘇曼殊
SU MANSHU

Spring Drizzles

I stand on the terrace playing my long flute in spring drizzles
Whence could I return home to watch the Qiantang tides in loud whistles
In straw sandals and holding a begging bowl my identity here is a nullity
In cherry blossoms how many bridges need I cross to declare my identity

春雨

春雨樓頭尺八簫
何時歸看浙江潮
芒鞋破缽無人識
踏過櫻花第幾橋

To the Hibiscus Temple at Fragrant Hill (1911)　　　古宋香水山芙蓉
寺題詩（1911）

I care for the perennial hunger and torment in motherland	已飢已溺是吾憂
To help uplift this common fate I had in years lent a hand	急濟心懷幾度秋
We rejoice in our culture the upholding of responsibilities	鐵柱幸勝家國任
And our traditional foundation helps us to ease the adversity	銅駝慢著棘荊遊
A thousand-year cable in decay often fails in suspension	千年朽索常虞墜
Devotion for duty once shown will not cease in action	一息承肩總未休
Who is in charge of shifts in winds and dusts since old	物色風塵誰作主
Just watch the falls how a central column mightily hold	唯看砥柱正中流

Written in Harmony with Comrade Guo Moruo (1944)

Looking back at the war clouds in the Southwest
High up the Erya Terrace our friendship is at its best
A thousand villages deserted in all three countries ancient
Four heroes lost twenty battalions in a single mission
To turn the north into a new rule we have plans definitely
Peace with our eastern neighbour now a high priority
Whence we cleared the civil war and foreign conflicts finally
I will engage you to drink our finest national brew heartily

和郭沫若同志登爾雅台懷人（1944）

回顧西南滿戰雲
台高爾雅舊情殷
千村倫落悲三楚
四位英雄喪廿軍
北國翻新看後勁
東鄰隰越可先聞
內憂外患澄清日
痛飲黃龍定約君

Passing the Wuyi Mountain (1961)

過武夷山（1961）

Over Mountain Wuyi to the other side	翻過武夷山
Beyond the hill another horizon comes in sight	山外別有天
Vernal breezes just arrived in wait	東風初到侯
Cold weather gone the warm south now in state	南地已無寒
Through the serene valley blue waters flow	綠水穿幽谷
Verdant woods embrace the huge mount in fold	青林擁巨川
We drove our car along the river bank	車行隨岸走
Where the scenery became new as we went	風景最新鮮

Enjoying the Yuexiu Garden (1961)

Flowers and trees fill the Yuexiu Garden scene
Hundreds of flowers bloom to vie for spring
Only the fragrance of the orchid stands out
It makes the Five-Goat City famous throughout

遊越秀公園（1961）

越秀公園花木林
百花齊放各爭春
唯有蘭花香正好
一時名貴五羊城

Singing for the Orchid (1961)

The serene orchid waits for winter to bloom

Its leaves green and verdant shine on the art screen

Early buds open gathering dews instantly fall

Its fragrance welcomes guests ten steps before they enter the hall

詠蘭（1961）

幽蘭奕奕待冬開

綠葉青蔥映畫台

初放素英珠露墜

香迎十步出庭來

Waiting for Rain (1963)

In a sky low with brisk winds no rain will arrive
Clouds and haze in the spheres lingering slight
The rains farmers love had gone with the wind
At dusk the sky remains bright a moon winks

望雨（1963）

風急天低雨不來
迷天雲霧自徘徊
農夫喜雨風吹去
臨夜晴明月色開

The Dragon Gate Grotto (1963)

龍門石窟（1963）

Out from the Dragon Gate the Yi River gently flows
Ancient relics on both banks richly show
Inside the grottoes relief carvings arts magic
Today they welcome visitors to appreciate

悠悠伊水出龍門
兩岸風光古蹟陳
石窟浮雕高美術
而今尚得動遊人

Remembering Comrade Chen Yi (1972)

For revolution you have devoted your entire life
With your coffin closed your deeds confirmed bright
To your teachers and the Way you showed respect
The roads you have travelled are rooted deeply in red

悼陳毅同志（1972）

一生為革命
蓋棺方論定
重道又親師
路線根端正

Tune: Waves Refining Sands–Passing Handan in Snow (1954)

Flying snows covering hills and rills
Keeping the plain pure
In spring warm airs we still feel cold
Green shoots in new crops welcome the blessing snow
People of all surnames celebrate the celestial show
In a group of one hundred a common interest shown
Inspecting scenes south of the river wherever
Gone is the Long March a decade in a click of fingers
Scenes and materials now new the world changed in surprise
Heaven and humanity ever so nice

浪淘沙·雪中過邯鄲（1954）

飛雪滿山川
淨化平原
融融暖氣卻春寒
嫩綠新苗逢瑞雪
萬姓同歡
乘興百人團
巡視江南
長征彈指十餘年
景物全新驚世變
天上人間

My Determination (1909)

Hot is the killing spirit in a world so ill
Inferior to powers ten thousand matters stand still
Duty bound I vow to keep motherland secured
Coming to study in Japan noble laurels not my will

述志（1909）

騰騰殺氣滿全球
力不如人萬事休
光我神州完我責
東來志豈在封侯

On Mountain Xuedou (1920)

This snow mountain what a serene sight
Three pools all wonders a scenic surprise
With woods and springs here I hold unity
Whence in success a hermit life here not a late destiny

雪竇山口占一絕句 (1920)

雪山名勝擅幽姿
不到三潭不見奇
我與林泉盟在夙
功成退隱莫遲遲

Thoughts at Changping Station (1925)

With three hundred student soldiers up front I lead
In this Eastern Campaign the cunning owls not rid
The revolution stranded in difficulty I alone irate
I thrust my sword skyward tears readily rain

常平站感吟一絕 (1925)

親率三千子弟兵
鴎鴉未靖此東征
艱難革命成孤憤
揮劍長空涕淚橫

To Review My Army Force—Two poems (1928)

The third of May is our national rancor
Losing a nation allows no one to leisure
Caring and truthful
Unite in one mind
Together we hurriedly strive
Revolution again revolution
Sacrifice more sacrifice
Black iron in red blood out
For motherland's independence equality and freedom
Independence, Equality, The Chinese Republic will be truly free

Concluding the Northern Expedition I stand unfulfilled
To quell our motherland's rancor is a man's will
Revolution is the only action to treat our national ills
Until a success in revolution to death I shall not sit still

出發校閱撰歌二則（1928）

五月三日是國仇
國亡豈許爾優遊
親愛精誠
團結一致
快來共奮鬥
革命革命
犧牲犧牲
黑鐵赤血

求我國家獨立平等與自由
獨立、平等，中華民國乃得真自由

北伐雖完志未酬
男兒壯志報國仇
報國復仇在革命
革命未成死不休

Touring Mountain Emei (1935)

Against the colours of dawn the sun rises
In gentle winds scripture chants murmur nigh
The snow mountain is cold since old times
For the Emei peak a unique shine
Up the Emei peak I climb
Leaving all worldly concerns behind
Visiting every temple I bear my mother in mind
Touring alone in my mother's mind

遊峨嵋口占二首（1935）

朝霞映旭日
梵貝伴清風
雪山千古冷
獨照峨嵋峯
步上峨嵋頂
強消天下憂
逢寺思慈母
望兒感獨遊

Reflection on Sixty-third Birthday (1949)

Sixty three years I lived in days trivial

Shames and failures endured

Neither regret nor wrath

No boasting no indolence

No remorse nor deceit

Self-sufficient and self-reflection

Lucky is this person

Grateful to God's affection

Meeting crisis and challenges

Self-awake and self-conscious

Striving to revitalize China

For Republic reconstruction

六三自箴（1949）

虛度六三

受恥招敗

毋惱毋怒

莫矜莫慢

不愧不怍

自足自反

小子何幸

獨蒙神愛

惟危惟艱

自警自覺

復興中華

再造民國

Four Principles for Self-advice (1950)
Self-empowerment in Natural Rules

四箴（1950）
法天自強

Nurture body and spirit in harmony and centrality	中和位育
Accept natural differences in man and woman variety	乾陽坤陰
Live truthfully in continuous activities	至誠無息
Spur the spirit to actualize cosmic possibilities	主宰虛靈
Expand virtue in keeping with heaven and earth	天地合德
Enshrine vision with the shines of sun and moon	主敬立極
Uphold respect in all scopes of humanity	日月合明
Contain personal desires and act righteously	克念作聖

Nurture Longevity in Happiness

Keep the mind pure and simple as uncultivated lands
Direct all instincts to achieve self-fulfillment
Treat life wide as wilderness and deep as ravine
As birds fly and fishes glide at ease
Swim leisurely and acknowledge the deeps
Be active and happy
Remember past and present to enrich self-sufficiency
Care for others with empathy

養天自樂

澹泊沖漠
本然自得
浩浩淵淵
鳶飛魚躍
優游涵泳
活活潑潑
勿忘勿助
時時體察

18

1887-1975
蔣介石
CHANG JIESHI

Revere Nature for Self-cultivation   畏天自修

See carefully and hear humbly	不睹不聞
Be vigilant and trustworthy	慎獨誠意
Be attentive and positive	戰戰兢兢
Be reserved and inhibitive	莫現莫顯
Pursue the ultimate truth with explorations	研幾窮理
Be kind and ready to be righteous	體仁集義
Develop self-respect and keep promises	自反守約
Exercise self-constrain and show propriety	克己復禮

Honour Nature to Fortify Self-confidence

事天自安

Keep the mind calm and the spirit growing	存心養性
Dwell on reasons in support of self-striving	寓理帥氣
Exercise innate potentials to challenge destiny	盡性知命
Integrate self with matters and cosmic activity	物我一體
Worry not and fear not	不憂不懼
Embrace The Way and adhere to Nature's leads	樂道順天
Do not boast nor practice deceit	無聲無臭
Be self-reliant as you approach your destiny	於穆不己

A Poem after Reading Newspapers (1945)

'Tis a pity to see flattering essays in the literary scene
People rush to doors of power for comforting inn
Freedom implies rules for writings of quality
Alas how many writers know not what is to be free

閱報戲作（1945）

弦箭文章苦未休
權門奔走喘吳牛
自由共道文人筆
最是文人不自由

In My Sick Bed on New Year's Eve (1945)

I shut my door early seeing rain and snow fly
Acres of abandoned land sit not a village thrive
Taking my family I know not where to settle in
Back to motherland I rejoice my country is surviving
Wars in the four seas keep my sick eyes blind
Nine years of suffering drags my spirit behind
What a joy to hear my daughter laughing by my bedside
Just as she appears in my dreams every night

甲申除夕病榻作時目疾頗劇
離香港又三年矣（1945）

雨雪霏霏早閉門
荒園數畝似山村
攜家未識家何置
歸國惟欣國尚存
四海兵戈迷病眼
九年憂患蝕精魂
扶牀稚女聞歡笑
依約承平舊夢痕

Remembering My Old Houses (1945)

The toll of bells heard faintly from afar
Thousands of crows roost in the forest shadows flatter
All my life I strive to reach where I am now at
Alone I have no kin in the four seas at this time of sunset
I greet our country's victory seeing hills and rills in ruins
In these remaining dreary hours and years I rid off worries
My old dwellings among pines and mums appear in all dreams
May as well accept my present place as where I had been

憶故居（1945）

渺渺鐘聲出遠方
依依林影萬鴉藏
一生負氣成今日
四海無人對夕陽
破碎山河迎勝利
殘餘歲月送悽涼
松門松菊何年夢
且認他鄉作故鄉

My Fifty-sixth Birthday (1946)

My eyes blinded last year a dead man was I
Living as man I was a ghostly sight
I laughed when my family held a birthday party for me
As if an oblate act to enliven an old dead man to be
Both ghostly and human homes care for feelings
Since antiquity book worms exaggerate moans of acrimony
My tearless eyes dry and my heart broken in pieces
I will not allow my writings to mislead future generations
My daughter in stress my wife sick what a pity
Years of fleeing and separation have hurt us deeply
How I wish peace comes and my sight is back with me
We will hold hands to sail home together a family

五十六歲生日三
絕乙酉仲夏五月
十七日（1946）

去年病目實已死
雖號為人與鬼同
可笑家人作生日
宛如設祭奠亡翁
鬼鄉人世兩傷情
萬古書蟲有歎聲
淚眼已枯心已碎
莫將文字誤他生
女癡妻病自堪憐
況更流離歷歲年
願得時清目復朗
扶攜同泛峽江船

075

陳寅恪
CHEN YINKE

Lantern Festival on Su Shi Rhymes (1947)

A dreary sky over ten thousand li of smokes from fights
To whom could the luminous moon direct her shine
Vigilant soldiers keep watch on top of city gate
Empty ships return their search for medicine but an ill fate
Symbolic animal dances on platforms keep people charmed
Poems conjure a sea of willows to weep for times gone
Festivities in Capital yore arouse dreams of shear bliss
How could I accept the fleeting passage of this New Year Eve

丁亥元夕用東坡韻（1947）

萬里烽煙慘淡天
照人明月為誰妍
觀兵已抉城門目
求藥空回海國船
階上魚龍迷戲舞
詞中梅柳泣華年
舊京節物承平夢
未忍匆匆過上元

New Year's Eve on Su Shi Rhymes (1950)

The sky is different on this side of the hill
A snowless winter sees no flower blooms still
Hills and rills are ready to knock on the spring door
My lot runs like a boat sailing on a waterless course
I pine for festivities of yore lying on a moon-flood bed
A blitz shatters my building column heralds in another new year yet
Folks in this river-side town remain in individual forlorn
Would anyone know a new century is set to march on

庚寅元用東坡韻（1950）

過嶺南來便隔天
一冬無雪有花妍
山河已入宜春檻
身世真同失水船
明月滿牀思舊節
驚雷破柱報新年
魚龍寂寞江城暗
知否姮娥換紀元

Random Thoughts on Way Back to China (1937)

Time is ripe for me to put aside writing to join the army
Leaving my wife and children behind is not easy
Away from my country for ten years tears and blood linger
Three days on board home I once again see red banners
Glad I am to bury my bones anywhere in my motherland
With this poem I weep to declare my patriotic intent
Four hundred million people sing in unison
With unbending will to fight the Jap dwarfs we are one garrison

歸國雜吟之二（1937）

又當投筆請纓時
別婦拋雛斷藕絲
去國十年餘淚血
登舟三宿見族旗
欣將殘骨埋諸夏
哭吐精誠斌此詩
四萬萬人齊蹈厲
同心同德一戎衣

Ascending Mountain Heng (1938)

Dragons battle in the central plain bloods drown my motherland
Each warlord attempts to claim his territory on hand
For the moment I rest my passions on the beauties of our hills and rills
My inner feelings pour on poems and essays like torrents under keel
Clouds cross ten thousand li of sky above spears held high
The sun shines on a thousand peaks where iron steeds ride
Here I find the ruins home of a Prime Minister of Tang Dynasty
Whence peace comes I shall visit his Emperor's hall of study

登南嶽（1938）

中原龍戰血玄黃
必勝必成恃自強
替把豪情寄山水
權將餘力寫肝腸
雲橫萬里長纓展
日照千峯鐵騎玻
猶有鄈侯遺跡在
寇平重上讀書堂

To Officials of Fengshun County (1965)

Thirty-eight years have passed in a flick of fingers
In all my dreams Chao An has always appeared
Towers cast shadows on waters containing the blue sky
Banners proudly fly waving red like burning tide
On receiving an order of great emergence one evening
The revolution up-rise spearheaded in a spirit burning
Today I revisit here to watch from the Golden Hill
The changed sun and moon shine on everything new

贈豐順縣委（1965）

彈指光陰卅八年
潮安每在夢中旋
樓台倒映涵虛碧
旗幟高揚似火燃
一夕湯坑書附羽
千秋英烈血噴煙
今來重到金山望
日月更新別有天

To My Father (1909)

Your son is determined necessary to leave this our ancestral village
I vow not to return until fame has become part of my vestige
One's bones could find a burial place anywhere seen
For a striving man hills everywhere are equally green

改西鄉隆盛詩贈父親（1909）

孩兒立志出鄉關
學不成名誓不還
埋骨何須桑梓地
人生無處不青山

Tune: Qin Garden Spring–Changsha (1925)

Alone I stand in the autumn cold
Turning north the Xiang River gently flows
Where the Orange Islet on behold
Ten thousand hills in crimson hue
Serial woods dyed in blazing red
Where blue waters reflect a crystal view
Hundreds of barges vie to get ahead
Eagles sour up the expanding sky
Fishes in the shallows happily glide
In this frigid world all creatures strive to be free
Brooding over this immensity
To the boundless land I ask
Who is in command of human destiny
Gathering here for reunion we a throng of peers
Vivid in memory are those busy vibrant years
In youth we studied side by side
Our lives and aspirations flowering high
By our bookish insight and ambitions
We boldly cast all restraints aside
To wage new grand plans to build a better nation
Using torrid words to set people afire
We condemned those powerful lords to mere muck in demise
Do you recall
How reaching midstream we met torrents so tall
Waves overtook our speedy boat

沁園春・長沙（1925）

獨立寒秋
湘江北去
橘子洲頭
看萬山紅遍
層林盡染
漫江碧透
百舸爭流
鷹擊長空
魚翔淺底
萬類霜天競自由
悵寥廓
問蒼茫大地
誰主沉浮
攜來百侶曾遊
憶往昔崢嶸歲月稠
恰同學少年
風華正茂
書生意氣
揮斥方遒
指點江山
激揚文字
糞土當年萬戶侯
曾記否
到中流擊水
浪遏飛舟

Tune: Buddhist Dancer–The Yellow Crane Tower (1927)

Wide wide flow the Nine Streams through our motherland
Deep deep the north and south is severed by a single thread
Misty rains blur the air amid a lingering haze
Tortoise and Snake hills hold the Big River in watchful gaze
Whither has the yellow crane gone
Only this tower saved keeping visitors in throngs
With my wine I drink to cheer the unceasing flow
My mind's tide swells high keeping the waves in hold

菩薩蠻 · 黃鶴樓 (1927)

茫茫九派流中國
沉沉一線穿南北
煙雨莽蒼蒼
龜蛇鎖大江
黃鶴知何去
剩有遊人處
把酒酹滔滔
心潮逐浪高

Tune: Moon Over West River–Jinggangshan (1928)

Flags and banners seen from foot of the hill
Up on hilltop sounds of bugles and drums continue
The enemy encircles us ten thousands round
Unmoved we calmly stand our ground
In forts and trenches our defence in good preparation
Determined to fight we are one-mind in action
From Huangyang Jie cannon fires sound thunder-like
Words arrive announcing the enemy had fled during the night

西江月·井崗山（1928）

山下旌旗在望
山頭鼓角相聞
敵軍圍困萬千重
我自歸然不動
早已森嚴壁壘
更加眾志成城
黃洋界上炮聲隆
報導敵軍宵遁

Tune: Picking Mulberries–Double-Nine Festival (1929)

Man's life ages easy the universe goes on
The Double-Nine Festival comes annually it is now on
Today it again appears
In the battleground yellow flowers their fragrance special
Once a year autumn winds blow powerful
Unlike spring song
Better than spring song
The universe bright with ten thousand li of frosts on

採桑子・重陽（1929）

人生易老天難老
歲歲重陽
今又重陽
戰地黃花份外香
一年一度秋風勁
不似春光
勝似春光
寥廓江天萬里霜

(The World in Total White) On the Guangchang Road (1930)

Our soldiers march on snowy grounds spirit high
Tall mountains loom overhead
We cross the Grand Pass in wild winds flags red
Whither we head
To Gan River terrain snow swept
On order of yesterday
Ten thousand workers and peasants march to Ji'an in haste

減字木蘭花・（漫天皆白）廣昌路上（1930）

雪裏行軍情更迫
頭上高山
風捲紅旗過大關
此行何處
贛江風雪迷漫處
命令昨頒
十萬工農下吉安

Tune: Buddhist Dancer–Dabaidi (1933)

菩薩蠻・大柏地 (1933)

Red orange yellow green blue violet indigo

赤橙黃綠青藍紫

Who is dancing with these colours in rainbow

誰持彩練當空舞

Th sun sets in slanting rays after rain

雨後復斜陽

The mountain pass in blues tinted

關山陣陣蒼

Fierce battles fought in those years in succession

當年鏖戰急

Village walls stood to bullet penetrations

彈洞前村壁

Thus decorated this mountain pass stands cheerful

裝點此關山

Today the holes look even more beautiful

今朝更好看

Tune: Serene Music–Huichang (1934)

Dawn is ready to break in the east
For me to begin my climb not too early
Crossing these blue hills will not make me old
The scenery here is just beautiful
Outside the city lofty peaks stand
To the East Sea the looming ranges extend
Our warriors march southward to Guangdong
This terrain green and lust richly shown

清平樂・會昌

東方欲曉
莫道君行早
踏遍青山人未老
風景這邊獨好
會昌城外高峯
顛連直接東溟
戰士指看南粵
更加鬱鬱蔥蔥

Three Poems of 16 Words (1934–1935)
(I) Mountain

I whip my horse to speed sitting on saddle

Look back in wonder

Three feet three from the sky I was under

十六字令三首（1934—1935）
（一）山啊

快馳駿馬沒有下鞍

驀然回首

僅離天三尺三

(II) Mountain

Roaring sea and river sent giant waves
Like steeds in an intemperate race
Ten thousand charge towards a battling place

（二）山啊

翻江倒海掀起狂濤
奔騰激越
如萬匹戰馬酣暢征戰

(III) Mountain

Peaks spear the green sky blades unworn
The sky seems to fall
But for the mountain column standing tall

（三）山啊

刺穿蒼天鋒刃依然尖銳
天似要塌下
雄峯卻獨撐其間

21

1893-1976

毛澤東

MAO ZEDONG

Tune: Remembering Qin Maid–The Loushan Pass (1935)

The west wind brisk

Under the frosty morning moon wild geese disquiet

The frosty morning moon

Horses' hooves sound like gentle breakings

Bugles not roar

The idle road along this grand pass an iron wall

With steady strides we are crossing the summit

Crossing the summit

The hills sea-blue

The setting sun blood-red

憶秦娥・婁山關（1935）

西風烈
長空雁叫霜晨月
霜晨月
馬蹄聲碎
喇叭聲咽
雄關漫道真如鐵
而今邁步從頭越
從頭越
蒼山如海
殘陽如血

Tune: Serene Music–Six Turn Mountain (1935)

Faint clouds hang in high sky
Southbound geese yonder fly
Whoever has not been to the Great Wall is not a true man tall
We have travelled twenty thousand li by a count of fingers
The peak up the Six-Turn Mount mightily high
Red banners flap in the west wind a great sight
Today long spears in our hands we hoist high
Whence will we have the mighty dragon tied

清平樂 · 六盤山 (1935)

天高雲淡
望斷南飛雁
不到長城非好漢
屈指行程兩萬
六盤山上高峯
紅旗漫捲西風
今日長纓在手
何時縛住蒼龍

To Comrade Peng Dehuai (1935)

Mountain high road far trench deep
Enemy army attacks in horizontal and vertical sieges
Who dares to ride a steed holding a big knife
But my General Peng Dehuai

六言詩・給彭德懷同志（1935）

山高路遠坑深
大軍縱橫馳奔
誰敢橫刀立馬
唯我彭大將軍

The Long March (1935)

The Red Army has no fear for the Long March trials
Leaguing ten thousand streams and hills is daily usual
Heavy gusts from the Five Ridges are but gentle breezes
And the grand Wumeng we tread like clay globules
The steep cliffs on the Jinsha is warmed by lapping waves
The Dadu iron-chain bridge is crossed with no regard for its cold
Mountain Min's snows a thousand li are greeted in delight
The three troops march on victorious their spirits high

長征（1935）

紅軍不怕遠征難
萬水千山只等閒
五嶺逶迤騰細浪
烏蒙磅礴走泥丸
金沙水拍雲崖暖
大渡橋橫鐵索寒
更喜岷山千里雪
三軍過後盡開顏

Tune: Remembering Palace Maid–Kunlun (1935)

念奴嬌 · 崑崙

（1935）

Across the sky you appear	橫空出世
Wild and fierce	莽崑崙
Witnessing all historic events in humanity	閱盡人間春色
Three million jade dragons fly in snow white	飛起玉龍三百萬
Spreading frigid colds all over the sky	攪得周天寒徹
Ice melts during summer	夏日消溶
Streams and rivers filled continuously chatter	江河橫溢
Men or fishes and turtles	人或為魚鱉
A century of successes and failures	千秋功罪
Who could give reasonable measures	誰人曾與評說
For Kunlun I can now say	而今我謂崑崙
Do not stand this tall	不要這高
Do not store so much snow	不要這多雪
How I like to draw my sacred sword against the sky	安得倚天抽寶劍
To cleave you into three slices	把汝裁為三截
One piece goes to Europe	一截遺歐
One for America	一截贈美
One stays here in Asia	一截還東國
A world in peaceful coexistence	太平世界
Warmth and cold we share equally	環球同此涼熱

Tune: Qin Garden Spring–Snow (1936)

The scenic charm of northern country
A thousand li of land frozen in ice
Ten thousand li of wilderness in snowdrift
North and south of the Great Wall
Rests an uncultivated domain looming
The Big River pours from its source to sea
Its winding course set on silent rolling
Mountain ranges dance like slithering silver snakes
The highland roams a spectra of elephant herds charging
All contend with the sky for stature
On a clear sunny day
Cladding in pure white and radiant red
The world's natural beauty finds no match
To a motherland of such awesome enchantment
Her sons and daughters bow to offer heroic feats
Alas regret the pioneer emperors of Qin and Han
Showed a lack of literary grace
The hailed leaders of the great dynasties Tang and Song
Had not much poetic imagination in their souls
And the Great Genghis Khan
Favoured son of Heaven in his day
Loved too much to bow down hawks for revelry
Gone are these heroes of history
When you seek men of abiding respect and true worth
Meet them today

沁園春·雪（1936）

北國風光
千里冰封
萬里雪飄
望長城內外
惟餘莽莽
大河上下
頓失滔滔
山舞銀蛇
原馳蠟象
欲與天公試比高
須晴日
看紅裝素裹
分外妖嬈
江山如此多嬌
引無數英雄競折腰
惜秦皇漢武
略輸文采
唐宗宋祖
稍遜風騷
一代天驕
成吉思汗
只識彎弓射大雕
俱往矣
數風流人物
還看今朝

The PLA Captures Nanjing (1949)

Over Mountain Zhong a heavy storm swept headlong
A million mighty soldiers have crossed the Yangtze River
This city of tiger and dragon now outpaced ancient glories
For a hopeful future heaven and earth have turned wittily
With unspent bravery we pursue the totting enemy
Not in search of idle fame those false heroes envy
If heaven pitied human miseries it would surely age
Towards a grand path of humanity we dare to race

人民解放軍佔領南京（1949）

鐘山風雨起蒼黃
百萬雄師過大江
虎踞龍盤今勝昔
天翻地覆慨而慷
宜將剩勇追窮寇
不可沽名學霸王
天若有情天亦老
人間正道是滄桑

Tune: Silky Sand Brook–Reply to Mr. Liu Yazi (1950)

The night long and dawn is late while red banners in suspense
For a century demons had enjoyed whirls in wild dance
People five hundred million strong failed to unite in their own land
With a single cock's crow Heaven and Earth are suddenly bright
Songs fill all corners of our nation including Yutian musical rites
And poets are inspired to sing their verses ever so high

浣溪沙·和柳亞子先生（1950）

長夜難明赤縣天
百年魔怪舞翩躚
人民五億不團圓
一唱雄雞天下白
萬方樂奏有於闐
詩人興會更無前

Tune: Wave Refining Sand–Beidaihe (1954)

浪淘沙 · 北戴河
（1954）

A heavy storm thrashes this northern land

White breakers leap up without end

No fishing boat off the Qinhuang Island

A boundless ocean appears not in my vision

Where have they gone

大雨落幽燕

白浪滔天

秦皇島外打魚船

一片汪洋都不見

知向誰邊

A thousand years of events

The Emperor of Wei wielded his long whip so proud

Standing on edge of East Sea he wrote poems resound

The same autumn wind is singing today

All human communities have changed

往事越千年

魏武揮鞭

東臨碣石有遺篇

蕭瑟秋風今又是

換了人間

Moganshan (1955)

I dash into this seven-seat van driving high
Turning to watch how mountain peaks roam in the sky
After turning forty-eight rounds of winding roads
We arrive at the Qiantang banks what a quick show

莫干山（1955）

翻身躍入七人房
回首峯巒入莽蒼
四十八盤才走過
風馳又已到錢塘

The Five-Cloud Mountain (1955)

五雲山（1955）

Rainbow colour clouds fly above the Five-Cloud sky
Linking far away peaks with the Qiantang Dyke nigh
Ask where the best scenery in Hangzhou lies
Here hear cuckoos singing in the wild

五雲山上五雲飛
遠接羣峯近拂堤
若問杭州何處好
此中聽得野鶯啼

Watching Hills (1955)

Thrice I climb up the northern peaks
Hangzhou appears in a glance so neat
Around the Phoenix Pavilion stand many trees
Peach flowers wave in the mountain breeze
I search for my fan in the heat
Feeling cold I ask my darling to meet
Like a leaf winding down from the sky
I welcome this nightingale in the twilight

看山（1955）

三上北高峯
杭州一望空
飛鳳亭邊樹
桃花嶺上風
熱來尋扇子
冷去對美人
一片飄飄下
歡迎有晚鶯

21

1893-1976

毛澤東

MAO ZEDONG

Tune: Prelude to Water Melody–Swim (1956)

水調歌頭‧游泳（1956）

Water of Changsha I drank moments ago	才飲長沙水
Fishes of Wuchang I now enjoy so	又食武昌魚
Across the Yangtze ten thousand li I swim through	萬里長江橫渡
On backstroke I search the sky for Chu State of old	極目楚天舒
Winds and waves no matter	不管風吹浪打
Just like pacing my courtyard in leisure	勝似閒庭信步
Today at ease	今日得寬餘
I hear Confucius by a stream said long ago	子在川上曰
How time incessantly flows	逝者如斯夫
A wall of sails in the wind	風檣動
Tortoise and Snake hills stand in	龜蛇靜
Grand plans in hold	起宏圖
Spanning north and south a bridge flies through	一橋飛架南北
Nature's deep chasm becomes a road	天塹變通途
On river west stands a cliff wall	更立西江石壁
Holding Mountain Wu's winds and rainfalls	截斷巫山雲雨
To create a calm lake up the gorges	高峽出平湖
Should the legend goddess stays watch	神女應無恙
She would marvel what changes are shaping our world	當今世界殊

Tune: Butterfly Loves Flower–Reply to My Friend Li Shuyi (1957)

I lost my beloved Poplar you lost your dearest Willow
Our loved souls will rise up the Nine Leagues for sure
Asking Wu Gang on the moon what is available
He readily serves his prized laurel brew
The lonely Moon Goddess swings her swift sleeves free
To dance for all loyal souls across the sky infinitely
On hearing news from earth that people have subdued the menacing tiger
Her joyful tears turn into mighty rain to fill the land with welcome water

蝶戀花 · 答李淑一（1957）

我失驕楊君失柳
楊柳輕颺直上重霄九
問訊吳剛何所有
吳剛捧出桂花酒
寂寞嫦娥舒廣袖
萬里長空且為忠魂舞
忽報人間曾伏虎
淚飛頓作傾盆雨

Watching the Tide (1957)

觀潮（1957）

Waves rolling in from a thousand li in tempest race

Snow white foams approach the Fisher Terrace

Mountains of people cheer for the grand view

Greeting the tides rise and recede like iron steeds fueled

千里波濤滾滾來

雪花飛向釣魚台

人山紛贊陣容闊

鐵馬從容殺敵回

Farewell to Plague Power (1958)
(I)

Blue rills and green hills not too many
Even our Hua Tuo had no power to rid off this pest tiny
Villagers fled in thousands leaving the land to waste
Ten thousand homes deserted where wild ghosts wail
As we sit the globe turns eighty thousand li a day
Surveying the universe I detect the Milky-Ways
Should the legend Cowherd question the Plague Power
The answer flows like a ceaseless river

送瘟神（1958）
（一）

綠水青山枉自多
華佗無奈小蟲何
千村薜荔人遺矢
萬戶蕭疏鬼唱歌
坐地日行八萬里
巡天遙看一千河
牛郎欲問瘟神事
一樣悲歡逐逝波

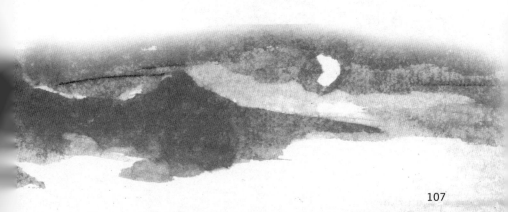

(II)

Willow tendrils wave in spring breeze in milliards	春風楊柳萬千條
Six hundred million Chinese wise as the ancient Yao and Shun	六億神州盡舜堯
Vintage rains swirl in our hearts like river torrents	紅雨隨心翻作浪
Our wishes carried forward on bridges in green mountains	青山着意化為橋
Silver hoes till grounds on the Five Ridges linking the sky	天連五嶺銀鋤落
Powerful arms quiver the Triple River flowing nigh	地動三河鐵臂搖
Where the Plague Power intends to dwell I ask	借問瘟君欲何往
To its demise sent by burning candles and paper barges	紙船明燭照天燒

（二）

Ascent to Lushan (1959)

A mount in flight perch towering the Big River banks
Up to the green crest my road twisted four hundred turns hence
Surveying the world beyond the ocean I keep my eyes cool
A hot wind spatters rains over the land through
The Yellow Crane appears afloat in the midst of nine streams
Billows roll on the eastern ancient countries white mists gleam
Who knows whither poet Tao has gone to
The land of Peach Blossom offers arable fields

登廬山（1959）

一山飛峙大江邊
躍上蔥蘢四百旋
冷眼向洋看世界
熱風吹雨灑江天
雲橫九派浮黃鶴
浪下三吳起白煙
陶令不知何處去
桃花源裏可耕田

Shaoshan Revisited (1959)

Vague dreams of separation I lament how time insistently goes
Thirty two years gone to my native home I again show
Red flags had incited serfs to take up arms for revolt
Despite despots their black whips held aloft
The sacrifice of lives helped to reinforce bold resolves
Peasants dared to invite sun and moon to change in cosmos
How happy I am to see rice and beans in fields thrive
At dusk heroes returning home where cooking smokes rise

到韶山（1959）

別夢依稀咒逝川
故園三十二年前
紅旗捲起農奴戟
黑手高懸霸主鞭
為有犧牲多壯志
敢教日月換新天
喜看稻菽千重浪
遍地英雄下夕煙

Reply to a Friend (1961)

Above Mountain Jiuyi white clouds sail high
The legend Prince on winds down green hills nigh
A single bamboo is stained by one thousand tear drops
Ten thousand clouds don on crimson clothes
Snowy waves in Dongting Lake surge up the sky
On Long Sands reverberating poems shake our minds
Untrammelled I am lost in perishing dream scenes
The hibiscus world aglow with the shine of dawn

答友人（1961）

九嶷山上白雲飛
帝子乘風下翠微
斑竹一枝千滴淚
紅霞萬朵百重衣
洞庭波湧連天雪
長島人歌動地詩
我欲因之夢寥廓
芙蓉國裏盡朝暉

Inscription on a Photo of Comrade Li Jin at the Fairy Cave (1961)

In the gloom of dusk I watch pines hardy

Riotous clouds sweep past in tranquility

Nature has given birth to a Cave for Fairies

Up the perilous peaks dwell scenes in endless variety

為李進同志題仙人洞照（1961）

暮色蒼茫看勁松

亂雲飛渡仍從容

天生一個仙人洞

無限風光在險峯

Tune: Song of Divination–Ode to the Plum Blossom (1961)

Wind and rain sent spring away
Snowflakes welcome spring back to stay
When icicles a thousand feet hang on cliffs high
There a single flower stands cute and bright
Cute and bright she intends not to possess spring alone
But content serving as harbinger for the first season
When the hills are filled with other flowers in bloom
She will smile in their midst satisfaction owned

卜算子・詠梅（1961）

風雨送春歸
飛雪迎春到
已是懸崖百丈冰
猶有花枝俏
俏也不爭春
只把春來報
待到山花爛漫時
她在叢中笑

Winter Clouds (1962)

Snow laden clouds like white cotton fluffs fly
Flowers on ten thousand trees scarcely thrive
In high sky cold waves sweep quickly
On earth warm air stays with gentle breezes
Our heroes are best duellers for tigers and leopards
None is afraid of big wild bears
Plum blooms love a time of whirling snow
Why wonder how flies freeze to death in total

冬雲（1962）

雪壓冬雲白絮飛
萬花紛謝一時稀
高天滾滾寒流急
大地微微暖氣吹
獨有英雄驅虎豹
更無豪傑怕熊羆
梅花歡喜漫天雪
凍死蒼蠅未足奇

Tune: Favouring the Groom Reading–History (1964)

Man and ape said goodbye in gesture polite
Through making stone tools thousands of times
Festivities behind
Bronze in hot furnaces created in delight
Who had matters guessed right
But for eons of years in cold and heat
Human history full of conflicts smiles deplete
In combat one another showed crescent bowing might
Time pass
Bloodshed in the wild

One page of historic record read in clear mind
In memory are words and bites
Lines of happenings gone by
Our finest kings and scholars showed their deeds
Keeping millions of passersby in deceit
How often heroes loyal to prosperity and happiness
In revolution to create benevolence and lasting fame
Braving total risks to wield a big axe golden
Singing on still
Dawn whites east

賀新郎・讀史
（1964）

人猿相揖別
只幾個石頭磨過
小兒時節
銅鐵爐中翻火焰
為問何時猜得
不過幾千寒熱
人世難逢開口笑
上疆場彼此彎弓月
流遍了
郊原血

一篇讀罷頭飛雪
但記得斑斑點點
幾行陳跡
五帝三皇神聖事
騙了無涯過客
有多少風流人物
盜蹠莊蹻流譽後
更陳王奮起揮黃鉞
歌未竟
東方白

21

1893-1976

毛澤東

MAO ZEDONG

Tune: Remembering Palace Maid–Two Birds Sing (1965)

念奴嬌 · 鳥兒問
（1965）

The legend bird Pang
covered nine thousand li with a flap of wings
Reaching the end of yonder ocean riding on winds
Backing the sky it makes a downward survey
Cities and human communities appear all his way
Gunfire continues with smoke covering the sky
Bullet showers leave holes on land far and nigh
Frightened a sparrow in the bush attempts to hide
To flit and fly it wishes to try

鯤鵬展翅
九萬里
翻動扶搖羊角
背負青天朝下看
都是人間城郭
炮火連天
彈痕遍地
嚇倒蓬間雀
怎麼得了
哎呀我要飛躍

Where to I enquired
To the jewelled palace up the hills of immortals
Do you not recall the autumn a year ago
A Triple Pack for Peace signed in moonshine

借問君去何方
雀兒答道：
有仙山瓊閣
不見前年秋月朗
訂了三家條約

Together with a meal of steaming potatoes
Adding beefs
No gut rumbles
Keep watch the world has changed a thousand fold

還有吃的
土豆燒熟了
再加牛肉
不須放屁
試看天地翻覆

116

Tune: Prelude to Water Melody–Revisiting Mountain Jinggang (1965)

水調歌頭 · 重上井崗山（1965）

To ride the clouds I have always aspired	久有凌雲志
Up Mountain Jinggang I again climb	重上井岡山
Coming ten thousand li to revisit this old place	千里來尋故地
Old territories appear in new faces	舊貌變新顏
Everywhere orioles sing and swallows glide	到處鶯歌燕舞
Streams bubble as they wind	更有潺潺流水
High roads meet the clouds in sky	高路入雲端
Once we crossed the Huangyang Jie	過了黃洋界
No perilous terrain lies	險處不須看
Winds and thunders stir	風雷動
Flags and banners fly	旌旗奮
Human activities comply	是人寰
It has been thirty eight years	三十八年過去
A moment in a snap of fingers	彈指一揮間
We can embrace the moon in the Ninth Sphere	可上九天攬月
And catch the Tortoise down the Five Seas	可下五洋捉鱉
To home singing victory at ease	談笑凱歌還
Nothing is impossible	世上無難事
If only we dare to scale high	只要肯登攀

Desires in Action (1966)　　　有所思（1966）

A time when unease is disturbing the Capital	正是神都有事時
I came south to seek plans inspirational	又來南國踏芳枝
Green pines express ideals piercing the sky	青松怒向蒼天發
Fading leaves drift with river flows in demise	敗葉紛隨碧水馳
A sudden thunder arouses the country into a stormy sea	一陣風雷驚世界
On all streets colourful banners parade to take siege	滿街紅綠走旌旗
I stand by the rail to watch the rapid rains	憑欄靜聽瀟瀟雨
People in motherland turn desires into action	故國人民有所思

Tune: Revealing Inner Feelings–To Zhou Enlai (1975)

In years gone by you served our motherland loyal
No fear for losing your head in the revolution
Today our country is red all through
To whom the prosperity be entrusted in good will
National construction still in progress
Body and soul in no rest
Grey hairs prolific
You and I and our future generations
Must we let our perennial aspirations
Go naturally with the eastern flow

訴衷情 · 贈周恩來同志 (1975)

當年忠貞為國籌
何曾怕斷頭
如今天下紅遍
江山靠誰守
業未就
身軀倦
鬢已秋
你我後輩
忍將夙願
付與東流

Written on Oil Cliff (1915)

My will a rainbow I sing my aspirations high
Before this I had followed revolutionary men with pride
Here I study to understand the rise and fall in history
I will work with my people towards universal equality

油岩題壁（1915）

放眼高歌氣吐虹
也曾拔劍角羣雄
我來無限興亡感
慰祝蒼生樂大同

Drinking in a Raining Night (1921)

Up the parlour in heavy rain 'tis time to drink high
Spirit warmed by wine on history and the four seas we opine
For revolution I devote with my sword drawn
To poetry I write with my brush on and on
Entering society I find myself but ordinary
Friends engaged relations are not extraordinary
In agitation I know not how to pass time
Roaring waves kept me awake past midnight

雨夜銜杯（1921）

雨撼高樓醉不成
縱橫豪氣酒邊生
會將劍匣拼孤注
又向毫錐泣綺情
入世始知身泛泛
結交儔侶尚平平
愁多無計尋排遣
澎湃聲傳鼓二更

Wishing Comrade Liu Bocheng a Happy Fiftieth Birthday (1942)

In the disciplined camps calm and alone
Gun shots and cannon fire mark our home
A general vital at fifty years old
You recently defeated the dwarfs deeds untold

劉伯承同志五十壽祝（1942）

細柳營中寂不嘩
槍垣炮堵即吾家
將軍五十人稱健
新得倭酋不自誇

In Harmony with a Poem by Comrade Zhu De (1943)

Did you sing the ancient victory song in echo
Reclaiming every inch of our lost hills and rills
I stop my steed outside the foggy Mountain Taihang
Wishing to sing with you the poetic tune of Dongzhou

和朱德同志詩 (1943)

將軍莫唱大刀頭
淪陷山河寸寸收
勒馬太行煙霧外
與汝同歌詠東州

At Qingdao (1954)

青島（1954）

In a corner a small house stands upright	小樓明一角
Amid green trees and shrubs it hides	深隱綠叢中
The sky a cover for the sea so wide	海闊天如蓋
Watching distant mountains this island is bear like	山遙島似熊
Gentle waves caress an old man holding a fishing line	輕波垂釣叟
At dawn he is a child playing with the tide	旭日弄潮童
The ancient Han Emperor's legacy comes to mind	忽憶劉亭長
How he sang the victory song mighty and high	蒼涼唱大風

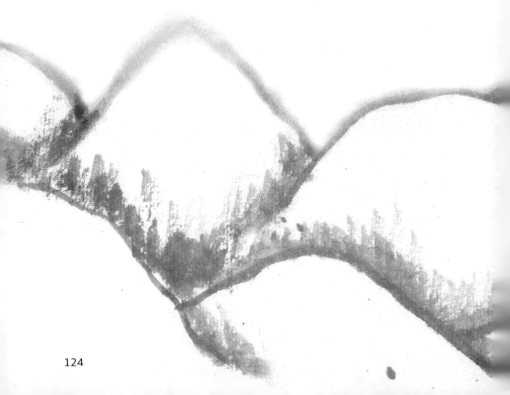

Visiting Gansu (1956)

The Western Corridor full of coal oil copper and iron ores
In history the ancients fought here in many wars
I stop to watch a forest of factories mirroring the sun
The shaded desert is home for melons and vegetables

遊甘肅（1956）

銅鐵煤油遍走廊
當年人道是沙場
佇看工廠林立日
戈壁蔭成瓜果鄉

22

1897-1986
葉劍英
YE JIANYING

Visiting Xinjiang (1956)

遊新疆（1956）

On his oxen Laozi gone from here to wherever

老子青牛去不還

In Tianshan today excavations in numbers ever

而今鑽探滿天山

Whence the railway arrives at this territory

自從鐵道通西域

Millions of youths come for new opportunities

百萬青年唱出關

The Yangtze River Bridge (1957)

The Tortoise and Snake hills guard on opposite sides
Perennial churning waves in midair fly
To submerge worn-out spears under sands
Testing how many heroic deeds hence
No count can depend

長江大橋（1957）

龜蛇對峙
千年濁浪排空起
折戟沉沙
英雄淘盡
都無覓處

127

Heaven Praises

天公歎服

This earthly immortal achieve

A long bridge of flying metals hangs

Spanning to connect every direction in motherland

地上神仙

長橋飛架

南北東西無阻

My thoughts go to the Galaxy up far

To see how the Weaver and Cowherd lovers are

With dismay and envy my heart beats fast

遙想銀河

斜窺牛女

端的乍驚還妒

I stand alone at mid-river

To behold Mountain Wu and Gorge Wu

Between the ancient divides of Wu and Chu

Now before me in full commanding view

江心獨立

看巫峽巫山

頭吳尾楚

任我從容指顧

Incessant waters flow independent

Boiling as they hurry to their eastward mission

流水不關情

讓它滾滾東去

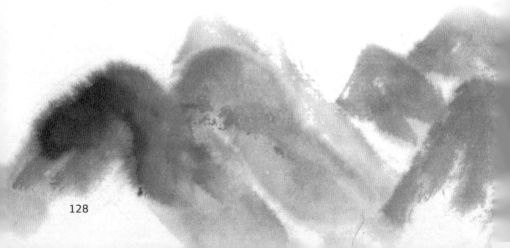

Back to Beijing from a Western Trip (1958)

On the plane home high above the seas
Thousands of miles of motherland seen in a cup of tea
On my finger tips the Great Wall extends to sea
In broad grins this returning son is so happy

由伯力返北京（1958）

天空海闊駕機回
萬里山河入酒杯
指點長城關競海
思歸人亦笑顏開

On Way Home from Visiting India (1958)

Monk Xuanzang travelled to India for years seventeen
Our present visit lasted days fourteen
Ask what ancient wisdom we have obtained
Words of friendship and neighbourliness papers contained

訪印度回國途中（1958）

玄奘西遊十七年
訪團往復四旬天
問君取得何經典
友誼鄉情紙滿篇

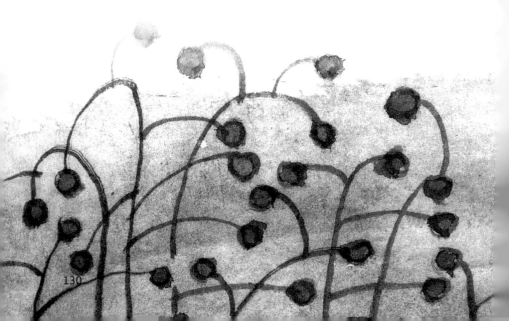

Passing Yangzhou at Qing Ming (1958)

I linger through the streets to find old books
Rubbing shoulders in crowds on papers we look
People say the shopkeepers are connoisseurs of words
I ask if they have watched human dramas global

清明由鎮江過揚州（1958）

閒踱街頭找古書
肩摩踵接笑睇餘
都稱老闆馬家到
我問君曾看戲無

Tune: Buddhist Dancer Pinning for Chopin in Warsaw (1958)

Warsaw looks beautiful autumn colours in gold
Chopin composed music in Paris till old
In winds waving willows sweep away the dying sun
I scratch my head to remember my home much fun
Flowers in spring compete to bloom in their finest
People compete to recite Chopin's music in their best
Sigh not for the dearth of real admirers
Maestro Boya regretted for his broken zither

菩薩蠻・華沙公園 懷蕭邦（1958）

金黃秋色華沙好
蕭邦作曲巴黎老
風柳掃殘陽
搔頭念故鄉
春來花競秀
遺曲人爭奏
莫歎少知音
伯牙悔碎琴

Tune: Butterfly Loves Flower–Hainan Island (1959)

A land afloat in the South Sea eon years old
All ups and downs seen through
Standing solid in support for the south sky
On top of the Five Finger Peaks night campers arrive
To secure the red district rule in years gone by
Su Shi wrote great poems here long ago
Palm trees stand tall as sky
Sweeping clean the sky no fog could hide
At Land's End edging the ocean today not as old
Celebrating good harvest people dance in folk songs manifold

蝶戀花 · 海南島（1959）

南海浮珠歷萬古
閱盡滄桑
挺作南天柱
五指峯高人宿露
當年割據紅區固
舊是東坡留句處
椰樹凌霄
掃盡長空霧
海角天涯今異古
豐收處處秧歌舞

At Deer Turn-Head Point (1959)   鹿回頭（1959）

The best time to gather beach shells is at dawn   海灘拾貝趁朝霞

Winds stir up waves carrying sands on   風捲浪堆沙

Up the hill top by the water edge I climb   境到登山臨水

To the far horizon my eyes and mind find   伊人望望天涯

Coconut milk quenches thirst fine   椰漿消渴

A drink of coffee brightens up the eyes   咖啡醒目

South-sea Island times merrily go by   南島韶華

A red bean twig on my hand   擷得一枝紅豆

I ponder to whom it be sent   思量寄與誰家

Tune: Butterfly Loves Flowers–On Yulin Port (1959)

The sun negates the cold spell to follow the eastward geese
Wind-blown snow is covering the mountain passes busily
Routs above the clouds witness the geese flying at ease
They arrive at Yulin by the ocean summer is already here
Summer and autumn separated only by three nights and days
At the Deer Return Point the beach is wide and cool
Red beans symbol of love are plentiful here for you
They veil the view of far horizon roads
In shallow waters blue fishes glide and playful
As if to mimic the legend Goddess of the Dragon Palace

蝶戀花 · 榆林港（1959）

日逐寒流尋雁去
風雪關山
不礙雲中路
飛到榆林天已暑
夏秋只隔三朝暮
到鹿回頭濱海處
紅豆離離
佔斷天涯路
淺水藍魚梭樣去
教人疑是龍宮女

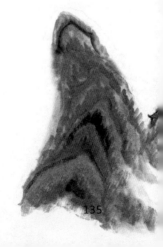

Thoughts at Eighty (1977)

At eighty I need not be concerned with successes and failures
There are plenty of successors to continue our revolution ventures
A great leader has drawn up this grand plan for our country
The young can spearhead with no hesitation building a new economy
A billion people join hands to rid off wrongs and create new deeds
Together with the world powers we stand or fall however we proceed
This old man enjoys singing for the colourful evening sky
All green hills in the sunset appear especially bright

八十書懷（1977）

八十毋勞論廢興
長征接力有來人
導師創業垂千古
儕輩跟隨愧望塵
億萬愚公齊破立
五洲權霸共沉淪
老夫喜作黃昏頌
滿目青山夕照明

On Top of Zhurong Peak

The view is unlimited on all sides
My coat flap is blown open by winds high
The roaring sounds in the pines invoke my fighting will
I vow to submit the invading dwarfs to kneel

登祝融峯

四顧渺無際
天風吹我衣
聽濤起雄心
誓盪扶桑兒

Singing for Li River

Vernal breezes escort my boat to lightly glide

Peaks walling the banks to supervise the welcoming treats

Galloping horses and painted cliffs are the great divides

At Xingping the beautiful scenes and I happily meet

詠灘江

春風灘水客舟輕

夾岸奇峯列送迎

馬躍華山人睇鏡

果然佳勝在興坪

Tune: For a Laugh–Scene of a Meeting

Heads heavy
Heads heavy
A four-hour long listening audience
Bodies bent eyes tired and guts empty
Peeping at the watch frequently
Watch peeping
Watch peeping
Monkey thoughts and steed images wandering

調笑令 · 會場素描

頭重
頭重
四個小時聽眾
腰斜眼倦腸飢
左手頻看計時
時計
時計
有點猿心馬意

Hotel Song Garden (1977)

Screened on four sides by hills so green
This garden hotel a paradise a retiree seen
Ten years of striving I should yet seek
Then home to hills and River Mei I shall read

松園（1977）

四面青山列翠屏
松園終不老閒身
會當再奮十年鬥
歸讀陰那梅水濱

On a Painting of Bamboo (1978)

Free brush moves like clouds to draw what is in mind
Hollow body and hard knots are models alive
What a wonder to know everything in life
Conquering difficulties and tests with pride

題畫竹（1978）

彩筆凌雲畫溢思
虛心勁節是吾師
人生貴有胸中竹
經得艱難考驗時

Visiting Home at Meixian (1980)

A brink of time in eighty years three
With a lamp by the window childhood memories glee
One hundred years of life approaching ninety
These evening hours shine bright and mighty

回梅縣探老家（1980）

八十三年一瞬馳
木窗燈盞憶兒癡
人生百歲半九十
萬丈霞光值暮時

Ten Poems at Goat City (4 verses) (1921)

(II)

羊石雜詠十絕
（四首）（1921）
（二）

Evening breezes cool the white walls east
I amble singing to rhyme with insect songs at ease
To count how many geese are returning I eye the sky
A single flowering branch shows at my bower nigh

晚風涼抹粉牆東
碎步微吟韻小蟲
為數歸鴻抬星眼
一枝春在小樓紅

(III)

（三）

Feeling free and leisurely I travel light
A single migrating bird up the tower high
Ten thousand lights and a sea of people seen at bay
Much like the legend lovers in the Milky Ways

乍逸閒情事薄遊
輕鴻飛上最高樓
明燈萬點人如海
恍惚銀河障女牛

(IV)

Approaching spring I ride to visit Ancient City out east
Ten thousand miles of pink flowers shine to please
I rein my horse to linger at the riverside pavilion near
Freeing my thoughts to roam with white clouds wherever

（四）

春來跨馬古城東
十里鶯花潋灩紅
鞭息徘徊亭畔路
統懷繚繞白雲中

(VI)

Brisk east winds sweep away haze in the evening
Kapok petals fallen no more flowers seen
Flute songs sounding flat much like cold tides
Away from taverns I see beautiful moonshine

（六）

颯颯東風掃暮霞
木棉落後更無花
簫聲咽似寒潮咽
不見秦樓見月華

Thoughts on a Spring Day (2 verses)
(1914)
(I)

I cast my eyes beyond the mountain greens
Thickening fog everywhere seen
Power struggles occupy the heartland in heat
Assassin strikes ceaselessly repeat

(II)

Cherry blossoms flush over a winding path
Green willows by the pond hush
Amid twitters of swallows
My thoughts spent another year will follow

春日偶成（二首）
（1914）
（一）

極目青山外
煙霾布正濃
中原方逐鹿
博浪踵相蹤

（二）

櫻花紅陌上
柳葉綠池邊
燕子聲聲裏
相思又一年

Seeing Pengxian Homebound (1916)

(I)

We met by chance predestination
Classmates in Tianjin not any accident
Your eloquence stuns even intimate friends
O'er wines and crabs we criticize every current event
Hardship and suffering we endure to rid off our foes
For our motherland no one is shy to fight and defend
Whence enemy gone we promise to turn to the land
Plots of land rented we will neighbour farm hands

送蓬仙兄返里有感（1916）

（一）

相逢萍水亦前緣
負笈津門豈偶然
捫虱傾談驚四座
持螯下酒話當年
險夷不變應嘗膽
道義爭擔敢息肩
待得歸農功滿日
他年預卜買鄰錢

(II)

As the east wind hurried passengers on board

We sang parting songs from the south shore

You will be a thousand li away in a twinkle

A dream souls tingle

Stars gone confirming separation regrets

Clouds dispersed sorrows stay intact

Fond are images of being together merry

We talked and wrote words never too many

（二）

東風催異客

南浦唱驪歌

轉眼人千里

消魂夢一柯

星離成恨事

雲散奈愁何

欣喜前塵影

因緣文字多

(III)

Our peers race to go home fast

You whipped your horse ahead of us

Although clumsy caring for things tiny

You excel in alacrity as you ride tides mighty

Crows choose to roost on thick leafy trees

Across the boundless sky a lone goose scours at ease

For friendship everlasting

Parting pains remain lasting

（三）

同儕爭疾走

君獨着先鞭

作嫁憐儂拙

急流讓爾賢

羣鴉戀晚樹

孤雁入寥天

惟有交遊舊

臨歧意悵然

No Title (1917)

The Grand River roared to resolutely turn back east
We searched for wise actions to better our nation not easy
Ten years I contemplated before a wall for a breakthrough
I will tread the seas and take any daring action essential

無題（1917）

大江歌罷掉頭東
邃密羣利濟世窮
面壁十年圖璧破
難愁蹈海亦英雄

Green Pine

Heavy snow loads down the green pine
The green pine stands upright fine
To know the lofty character of the pine tree
Wait until the snow thaws and disappears

青松

大雪壓青松
青松挺且直
要知松高潔
待到雪化時

Wishing Commander Zhu De a Happy Sixtieth Birthday (1946.11)

The high peak of Mountain Tai leads ten thousand hills
Your virtues of wide tolerance like seas and rills
Serving the people continuously for thirty years
We all look forward to being with you for ten more years

祝朱總司令六旬大慶（1946 年 11 月）

高峯泰嶽萬山從
大海盛德在能容
服務人民三十載
七旬會見九州同

Poems for Plum Mount

(I)

You chop off my head today I say ordinary

A hundred battles not enough to create a new country

I go now to mourn the souls of comrade martyrs

And dispose the Death Lord hoisting ten thousand banners

梅嶺三章

（一）

斷頭今日意如何

創業艱難百戰多

此去泉台招舊部

旌旗十萬斬閻羅

(II)

The south has been under fires and smokes for ten years
Hung high in the Capital this my head will surely appear
My surviving comrades will fight to win our cause
Victory news will fly like celestial oblations for lives lost

（二）

南國烽煙正十年
此頭須向國門懸
後死諸君多努力
捷報飛來當紙錢

(III)

Joining the revolution is our home
Bloody rains and smelly winds are endured for a goal
To die for a noble cause benefiting the people is a daily reality
Among our people we pledge to plant flowers of liberty

（三）

投身革命即為家
血雨腥風應有涯
取義成仁今日事
人間遍種自由花

24

1901-1972

陳　毅

CHEN YI

Remembering My Wife (1932)

On hills under the yellow spring how are you

Among papers you left are poems in view

Your images alive on pages here and there

By the door I seem to see a cold beauty hither

Among papers you left are poems in view

Whenever I read them I am with you

Compare to heaven earth is a better place to be

With you in wedlock my wish has become real

By the door I seem to see a cold beauty hither

The shadows gone I know not whither

Home from your funeral a cold moon this night

On hills under the yellow spring how you might

People say revolution is a life so good

Devotion to the army death a noble toot

Hardship and confinement are days so normal

Losing spouse at mid-age tears torrentially flow

憶亡（1932）

泉山渺渺汝何之

檢點遺篇幾首詩

芳影如生隨處在

依稀門角見玉姿

檢點遺篇幾首詩

幾回讀罷幾回癡

人間總比天堂好

宿願能償連理枝

依稀門角見玉姿

定睛知誤強自支

送葬歸來涼月夜

泉山渺渺汝何之

革命生涯都說好

軍前效力死還高

艱難困苦平常事

喪偶中年淚更滔

Climbing Mountain Dayu (1935)

Above Mountain Dayu the sky hangs low in the eve
European and Asian affairs seen in misty unease
Bits of our motherland a traitor had sold
Defence flames burn all over red flags uphold

登大庾嶺（1935）

大庾嶺上暮天低
歐亞風雲望欲迷
國賊賣盡一抔土
彌天烽火舉紅旗

On My Thirty-fifth Birthday (1936)

Going west our army spirit like a rainbow
Beneath the south sky a battle again unfold
Half of our motherland is in a bloody sea
Many a bosom friend killed and buried beneath
Searched in days and attacked by night we survived
Ten thousand dead and wounded as ghosts we are alive
Tested to the limits events must surely change
Whence heaven and earth turns motherland crimson

三十五歲生日寄懷（1936）

大軍西去氣如虹
一局南天戰又重
半壁河山沉血海
幾多知友化沙蟲
日搜夜剿人猶在
萬死千傷鬼亦雄
物到極時終必變
天翻地覆五洲紅

Field Camps (1936)

Threshing rain in harsh winds no home possible
Day after day our field camps move with war vehicles
Cold foods fill our guts hunger remains all day
We quash louses silently wild flowers we face
Stones however small can fill up a bloody sea
We wish our soldiers luck crossing the Jinsha River
In dark nights we can see leaving lamps behind
The legendary judge his noble deeds kindle our minds

野營 (1936)

惡風暴雨住無家
日日野營轉戰車
冷食充腸消永晝
禁聲捫虱對山花
微石終能填血海
大軍遙祝渡金沙
長夜無燈凝望眼
包胥心事發初華

Fire Parade on Evening of New Year's Day (1938)

We welcome the new year singing and drunk on way home
The sky red with ten thousand framing torches in hold
Citizens and soldiers in joint celebration a big event in motherland
We will win the defence war soon to exalt peace on this land

元夜火炬遊行（1938）

歸來大醉歌元夜
火炬燒天擁萬人
如此軍民邦國盛
待看戰勝保和平

The New Year Banquet (1939)

In smart uniform friends fill up the hall
Ears red after few drinks we loudly call
After three years of war we enjoy ourselves today
The enemy defeated the Capital is ours without delay

元旦公宴 (1939)

峨冠博帶朋滿座
耳熱酒酣意氣豪
三年抗戰今朝樂
破敵收京賴我曹

Boating Eastward on the Lake (1939)

Beneath Mountain Jingting oars on my skiff gently sing
Rains keeping sky and water misty I travel like dreaming
Would I meet the spirits of poets *Li and Xie herein
Ten thousand years of concerns reflected in ripples' gleam

*Poets Li Bai (701-762, Tang Dynasty) and Xie Tiao (464-499, Southern Dynasties)

由宣城泛湖東下 (1939)

敬亭山下櫓聲柔
雨灑江天似夢遊
*李謝詩魂今在否
湖光照破萬年愁

Wedding Day (1940)

Red candlelight waves to greet this happy day
Undoing your make-up you busy with poetry
How grand it is our hearts join could this be a dream
Eyes meet in silence our love showing in gleams
In a smile we put all past hardships away
We vow to love with mutual support in future days
We kiss to tell one another ours is a hundred-year affair
The moon peeps in at late night her well-wishes fair

佳期（1940）

燭影搖紅喜可知
催妝為賦小喬詩
同心能償渾疑夢
注目相看不語時
一笑艱難成往事
共盟奮勉記佳期
百年一吻叮嚀後
明月來窺夜正遲

A Will–By a Wounded Female Comrade (1940)　記遺言（1940）

A revolutionary sheds blood but not tear　　　　　　革命流血不流淚

Living and dead uncertain imbuing no blame or fear　生死尋常無怨尤

Blood flows like Yangtze currents never ends　　　　碧血長江流不盡

A promise in nine vessels will last years hundreds of tens　一言九鼎重千秋

Waiting for My Wife Home from East (1941)

Your footsteps ring in my ears incessant
Knowing your travel in trouble I dream for a solution
Listening to the time dripper at dawn
The moon bears witness to my anxious concerns

內人東來未至——
夜有作（1941）

足音常在耳間鳴
一路風波夢不成
漏盡四更天未曉
月明知我此時情

Thoughts on the Fifth Anniversary of Japanese Invasion (1942)

Today marks the difficult war against the Japanese invasion
Increasing new tombs inspire me to find a viable solution
Five years of bloodshed awake people in our motherland
Sons and daughters defended our Han tradition at length
We tolerated a child-emperor on a false throne
Fighting between siblings readily condoned
People struggle to gain a basket offering nine measures of hills
All of our billion people will rise to eliminate the common foe

"七七" 五週年感懷（1942）

即今抗戰艱難日
累累新墳啟我思
五年碧血翻滄海
一片丹心照漢旗
國中忍見兒皇立
朝內惟謀萁豆炊
九仞為山爭一簣
同仇敢與億民期

On Willow Lane in Spring (1943)

On Huai River's mid-course stands a land full of willows
Smooth sands and green fields assure tendrils gently flow
Leisurely I test my steed this fine day of spring
How often is life free as a gull exempt from strain
With affection we drink to say adieu to spring
Incessant winds and rains hurry her leaving
Beautiful scenes in humanity exist everywhere
Pear flowers in piles before our eyes appear
Along ten li of the Huai I walk by the moon late at night
Lanterns ablaze inspire affective thoughts nigh
Singing old songs we laugh to our hearts content
Our eyes bright with new battle hymns attained

大柳巷春遊（1943）

淮水中分柳巷洲
平沙綠野嫩絲抽
春郊試馬優遊甚
難得浮生似白鷗
為惜春殘共舉杯
番番風雨苦相催
人間好景隨時在
滿眼梨花錦作堆
十里長淮步月遲
闌珊燈火啟情思
舊歌不厭人含笑
抗戰新聲更展眉

163

Night Watch at the Huai River (1943)

Willows standing on glittering sands in the evening hue
Above the Huai River cranes compete to fly in my view
Watching hill-like clouds expanding in the wide sky
How I wish to ride a whale to conquer waves to go home

淮河晚眺 (1943)

柳岸沙明對夕暉
長天淮水鶩爭飛
雲山入眼碧空盡
我欲騎鯨跋浪歸

Passing Through Marshy Lake (1943)

Our skiff speeds forward under a sky clear from pollute
Above the lake the evening sky a glowing rouge
Passing through the sandy waters we wake up birds roosting
At dawn my white steed and I pace the willowy bank so pleasing

過洪澤湖（1943）

扁舟飛躍趁晴空
斜抹湖天夕陽紅
夜渡淺沙驚宿鳥
曉行柳岸雪花驄

Crossing the Old Yellow River (1943)

A thousand li of sand marks the ancient Yellow River course
In passing I search for lodging times three or four
Drizzles all evening I sleep not at all
Behind window all night I count snow flakes fall

再過舊黃河（1943）

故道黃河千里沙
旅途投宿二三家
黃昏細雨人不寐
黈夜隔窗數雪花

Going West of Mountain Taihang Stranded in Snow (1944)

To Mountain Taihang westward I cross
Favoured snow from heaven falls
Silver vessels crown the peak
Down deep valley fertile fields sit
I urge my steed it refuses to proceed
Stranded in a mountain village I'm alone indeed
Who knows when the ice would melt
Our march thus forced to quell
At night I ponder facing a dim wall
Many shadows shift ending in harmony
The dying lamp red lights flicker
Beating snow penetrates the window paper
My cold quilt helps me not to dream
Writing poems good thoughts stream
Fervently I sing for Mountain Taihang mighty
Who could stop my will to strive widely
Ending my songs I pray for dawn
One whip my steed jumps over River Fen

由太行山西行阻雪 (1944)

我過太行山
瑞雪自天墮
高峯鑄銀鼎
深谷擁玉座
策馬不能行
山村徒枯坐
冰雪何時融
征程從此錯
夜深對暗壁
搖搖影自和
殘燈不成紅
雪打窗紙破
衾寒難入夢
險韻詩自課
浩歌賦太行
壯志不可奪
歌罷祝天曉
一鞭汾河過

Tune: Yu the Beautiful–Spring Night (1944)　　虞美人・春夜（1944）

Up in cliffy mountain in spring sleep unease	料峭春寒人不寐
Dogs in the village bark incessantly	村犬聲聲吠
More than once I get up to light a lamp	幾番推枕起挑燈
A sky of stars flicker a moon luminous	戶外星光冉冉月華生
A traveller's yearning far and free	遊絲萬丈應難系
His dream reaches a thousand li	客夢波千里
He arranges his baggage and sits to worry	一番檢點一番愁
A slap in the head by a Chan master makes him happy	恰似禪家棒喝正當頭

An Evening Walk at Hot Spring (1956)　　溫泉晚步（1956）

Arriving at Stream Hill a scenic resort ultimate　　來到溪山絕勝處

Arranging inkwell and brush my home is made　　安排筆硯即為家

After watching the waterfall the day turns into eve　　看罷瀑布天色晚

Slowly the moon ascends shining river sands in relief　　緩緩戴月走溪沙

Guangdong (1957)

The Goat City stands overlooking a big plain
Layers of vegetation and woods loaming green
Flowers and shrubs thrive in spring in all seasons
A thousand years of Tang language and Cantonese vision
Foreign ships in a century invade creating calamity
Poets over the ages their works rich in creativity
Grand is this revolution by the common people
The hills of Yellow Flower and Red Flower burials
Where the Pearl met the ocean twenty thousand years ago
Today's Pearl Delta a land fertile for all vegetation growths
The White Cloud Hill and the Lychee Bay witness waters green
Villages feature flowers and trees their fragrance in the wind
The Chao-Shan districts are famous for agricultural production
The Ancient Pass north houses minerals awaiting excavation
A hundred tribes had converged to thrive in this beautiful land
Today's new construction by the people a luminous trend

廣東（1957）

高閣羊城接大荒　　　二萬年前此海口
騁懷極望鬱蒼蒼　　　而今沖積匯珠江
四時春氣榮花木　　　白雲荔灣山水綠
千載唐音聽粵腔　　　芳村花地草木香
海舶百年來禍患　　　潮汕農產千斤縣
謫人歷代富篇章　　　連韶礦藏億噸量
最是人民革命好　　　百粵自來形勝地
黃花崗連紅花崗　　　人民建設更生光

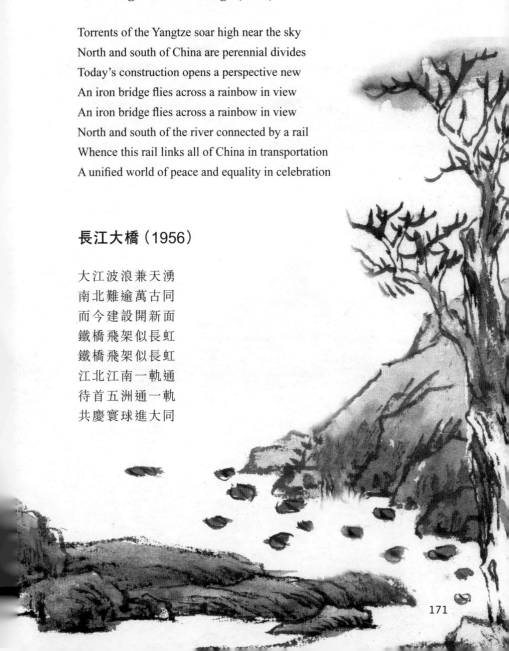

The Yangtze River Bridge (1956)

Torrents of the Yangtze soar high near the sky
North and south of China are perennial divides
Today's construction opens a perspective new
An iron bridge flies across a rainbow in view
An iron bridge flies across a rainbow in view
North and south of the river connected by a rail
Whence this rail links all of China in transportation
A unified world of peace and equality in celebration

長江大橋（1956）

大江波浪兼天湧
南北難逾萬古同
而今建設開新面
鐵橋飛架似長虹
鐵橋飛架似長虹
江北江南一軌通
待首五洲通一軌
共慶寰球進大同

The Su Dyke on West Lake (1964)

East of West Lake I tour in the morning glow
A clear sky mirrors water lilies in tender yellow
Rowing my skiff oars swift the Su Dyke appears
Both man and scenery seen in a painting so clear

遊蘇堤（1964）

日曜晨遊湖之東
嫩黃荷葉映晴空
乘船打槳蘇堤望
彼此均在畫圖中

Tune: Butterfly Loves Flower–Kathmandu Seen in the Morning (1965)

The Capital a serene beauty after a wash by rain
The sun's rays caress all of it in the morning
A touch of pale fogs arrive and go away
The mountain nests green tops and cliffs in grey
Pink walls and golden pyramids decorate verdant forests
Our diplomat to East Asia visits cities of interest
Noble hosts greet humble guests
They exchange present challenges and future quests
The Mahabharata a link between earth and heaven
Our friendship surpasses its heights beyond assessment

蝶戀花 · 加德滿都晨望（1965）

雨後雄都清又麗
梳掠朝陽
薄霧飛還聚
翠嶺蒼崖圍素壁
紅垣金塔穿林際
東使一行千萬里
賢主嘉賓
意厚談能細
喜馬拉雅天接地
友情飛越高難計

No Title

All heroes love beauties since old
Not all beauty lovers are mighty and bold
Though a hero I am not
I love beauties as a hero ought

無題

自古英雄多好色
好色未必皆英雄
吾輩雖非英雄漢
唯有好色似英雄

Touring Huashan

I gaze far eastward from the Great Wall
The same hills and rills my Governor reigns not
Sources of deep hatred and anger must be retorted
In armours I will return home victory songs resonant

遊華山感懷

極目長城東眺望
江山依舊主人非
深仇積憤當須雪
披甲還鄉奏凱歸

On Top of Huashan

I come by chance and forget to return home

Scenes as familiar as in happy dreams roam

Remembering my birthplace my heart is shattered

The master had changed though hills and rills remain here

詠華山

偶來此地竟忘歸

風景依稀夢欲飛

回首故鄉心已碎

山河無恙主人非

Elder Liu Visits Me in Taiwan

For ten years I ill not an instant
Old friends have not left me distant
This life surviving war and seizure
Reading quietly remains my only pleasure

柳老渡台來訪

十載無多病
故人亦未疏
餘生烽火後
唯一願讀書

26

1902-2003
蘇步青
SU BUQING

Gazing Afar from the Love Hill Pavilion (1940 riding home)

I linger on this Love Hill Pavilion in childhood days
Watching villagers work and rest in so many ways
Riding home on my cow's back before the sun sets
Through narrow winding paths the hills quiet
Clouds pass giving thousands of pictures of wind and rain
Streams sing as summers go and autumns come to reign
I've always loved spring when fragrant green pastures weave
And welcome returning boats to moor on piers in eves

南雁蕩愛山亭晚眺（1940 年回鄉）

愛山亭上少淹留
煙繞村耕欲漸休
牛背只應橫笛晚
羊腸從此入山幽
雲飛千嶂風和雨
灘響一溪夏亦秋
長憶春來芳草遍
夕陽渡口繫歸舟

Visiting Double Seven Pavilion (1944)

I climb up the path wearing thin clothes
Lantern in hand all the way through
Trees stand along the road on vigil
By riverside the Double Seven Pavilion stands true
Travelling great distance I grow old
My homeland green hills I dream to behold
Gazing north could tears not roll
Bloods all over the central plain from wars old

遊七七亭（1944）

單衣攀路徑
一杖過燈汀
護路雙雙樹
臨江七七亭
客因遠遊老
山是故鄉青
北望能無淚
中原戰血腥

Half an Acre (1945)

On half an acre of fields with sunshine plenty
To grow vegetables for food is a wish of my family
Meandering streams help to drain excessive rains
Seeding heavy we keep shoots a distant from pig raids
Who can predict how harvests turn out fat or lean
We cultivate together not expecting to win
A hermit's life is my fondest desire
I shall pass my old age shouldering moonshines ever

半畝（1945）

半畝向陽地
全家仰菜根
曲渠疏雨水
密柵遠雞豚
豐歉誰能卜
辛勤共爾論
隱居那可及
擔月過黃昏

**Tune: Remembering the Qin Maid–
Returning Home from Taiwan (1946)**

Taiwan Strait
On the deep blue ocean tidal songs quiet
Tidal songs quiet
My lonely airplane points far
To China coast cities north and east of the river

Where clouds disperse mountain ranges roam
On the vast clear sky 'tis time to go home
'Tis time to go home
Red towers I know
Hard bean flowers white as snow

憶秦娥・從台歸國
（1946）

台灣峽
深藍一片波聲歇
波聲歇
孤機遙指
浙東甌北

白雲開處山重疊
晴空萬里歸時節
歸時節
紅樓幽夢
菱花新雪

Sharing a Meal with Feng Zikai (1947)

Happy moments together we delight in sharing simple dishes
Do not let fuel and rice cause us any distress
Vernal breezes are greening the grass in front of our door
Let us endure the remaining cold to see winter no more

夜飲子愷先生家賦贈（1947）

草草杯盤共一歡
莫因柴米話辛酸
春風已綠門前草
且耐餘寒放眼看

Visiting Eastern Europe (1956)

I left the Capital flying north at dawn
The Great Wall comes to view as I travel on
Sands and rocks connect the frontiers in harmony
Around the clear lakes communities thrive water plenty
My thoughts on humanity roam far yet near
Before me clouds and trees pass by in autumn sphere
Cool winds keep the evening sky clear and bright
Rousing feelings for motherland miles and miles

訪東歐（1956）

朝別京師向北行
卻從機上望長城
平沙遙接塞疆合
巨邑獨臨湖水清
疇昔天涯今咫尺
眼前雲樹半秋聲
涼風吹澈晴空暮
喚起相思萬里情

Moaning My Colleague Chen Jiangong (1957) (I)

悼念陳建功（1957）
（一）

I sing alone on our strivings and deeds together
Seeing tavern banners with you again whither
I wish for government support to teach more students
To help them find their own roads in confidence

武林舊事鳥空啼
故侶凋零憶酒旗
我欲東風種桃李
於無言下自成蹊

(II)

A new song blares out hope from the high tower
On the bridge of practicality you and I were together
Who else in this world is pursuing our shared goal
My dream goes to Hangzhou imagination holds

（二）

清歌一曲出高樓
求是橋邊憶舊遊
世上何人同此調
夢隨煙雨落杭州

Old Steed (1972)

Red mane and black tail enduring many years and moons
Up and down the motherland you left your trots in tunes
Your four legs trot with imagination morning and night
Sure of your direction to travel a hundred years you aspire
Your ears are plucked to the clouds for movement sounds
Your mind set to trotting for miles away from the manger bounds
The ancient Noble King vied paradise in the horizon
Who needs to scorn the west wind in healthy conditions

老馬（1972）

黑尾紅鬃歲月侵
神州異域幾登臨
四蹄想像霜晨月
識途猶抱百年心
雙耳悠揚雲外音
伏櫪未忘千里志
穆王逝矣瑤池遠
莫對西風起暮吟

To My Student (1972)

At Guizhou thirty years ago
On a different idea I challenged you
Old today in Shanghai I set up my lectern
How happy to see you so independent

給張素誠 (1972)

三十年前在貴州
曾因奇異點生愁
如今老去申江日
喜見故人爭上游

Guizhou (1977)

'Tis early fall here in the village by riverside
Under bamboo shade stands my hut alone and fine
Waves of thriving wheat flow in thousand fields
A herd of homebound cows walking at ease
People exchange views on worldwide events
Letter from friends lost in movements of pretence
When will this disarray turn into satisfaction smiles
Away here ten thousand miles I exist in the wild

貴州（1977）

江村落木初
修竹蔭孤廬
麥秀風千畝
牛歸雨一墟
客談天下事
潮送故人書
亂定知何日
投荒萬里餘

To My Wife Our Gold Jubilee (1978)　　金禧給妻（1978）

Our love deepened following cherry blooms　　櫻花時節愛情深
Ten thousand miles we together come home　　萬里迢迢共度臨
Grey hairs on your beautiful face only natural　　不管紅顏添白髮
Our golden jubilee values more than gold　　金婚佳日貴於金

Watching the Jinmen Islands (1981)

I come south to the Egret Island when autumn is full
Looking east from this dangling platform thoughts roam
Why should this tiny strand of water before my eyes
Divide my motherland like ten thousand hills far and high

望大小金門島（1981）

鷺島南來秋正濃
危台東望思無窮
為何衣帶眼前水
如隔蓬山一萬重

Remembering My Native Home (1983)

Away from this famous mountain forty years gone
Frequent thoughts to return float on clouds in sky southern
The Immortal Queen is happy with so many offerings
The ancient saint his profound essays distinct
I used to ride on my cow daily playing a bamboo flute
Through winding paths to reach home wetting no foot
How lovely good wishes flow easy in the community
Pink oranges and yellow tangerines feature many villages

憶故鄉（1983）

一別名山四十春
有時歸思寄南雲
仙姑何幸馨香火
孫老無端榜會文
牛背笛橫斜日渡
羊腸徑逐故園門
秋來處處堪留戀
朱橘黃柑又幾村

A Century of Love (written in 2002, 100th birthday)

To the yonder world you have quietly gone

In my empty study I pine for you nights on and on

Through many difficulties we stayed together for life

Even age one hundred togetherness will not forever thrive

By lamplight I recall you busy keeping our house clean

My tears incessant you will not see at Yellow Spring

I will pick a dewy flower tomorrow morning

And place it before your likeness kind and serene

世紀絕戀（寫於 2002 年百歲生辰）

人去瑤池竟渺然

空齋長夜思綿綿

一生難得相依侶

百歲原無永聚筵

燈影憶曾搖白屋

淚珠沾不到黃泉

明朝應摘露中蕊

插向慈祥遺像前

In Praise of Tao Qian

You bow not to work for a government salary
Returning free to write new style poetry
The moon shines on daisy fences ringing flute songs
Peach flower petals ride the spring stream to float on
Your narration genuine and clearly romantic
Historic remarks profound and spirited
Only if your honour lived in a prosperous society
Why would you have to be a hermit or nobody

頌陶小詠

不為五斗折腰身
歸去來兮辭賦新
籬菊曾馨三徑月
桃花猶泛一溪春
行文爽朗而瀟灑
詠史激昂如有神
倘使先生逢盛世
何須高隱作閒人

Returning Home from the Bun

Light rain pours silver drizzles at the pier

Miles of plane trees shade hundreds of families

On this spot I left to go abroad years ago

With a simple suitcase to dream for a future colourful

外灘夜歸

渡頭輕雨灑銀花

十里洋桐綠萬家

正是當年停泊處

布衣負笈夢榮華

Zhejiang University

Returning to the university spring has arrived
Learning flows like singing streams in halls bright
Tens of thousands of winds and rains had come and gone
Here in the south-east this mountain stands for excellence
Sky high old trees give shades to the Grand Hall
Bathing in the fragrance are scholars from many shores
Do not idle around the mountain gate to guess the future
No second peak of wisdom will appear without nurtures

浙江大學

重到武林春已闌
如來殿下水潺潺
千風萬雨都過盡
依舊東南第一山
古木參天寶殿雄
萬方遊客浴香風
勸君休坐山門等
不再飛來第二峯

A Happy Eightieth Birthday Wish to a Friend

Life's supreme wish is to enjoy all brightness when old
To regard eighty years as eighteen years old
Being healthy who cares if grey hairs appear
A flourishing life style its secret readily shared
Three years of poetic thoughts generate many dreams
The Four Modernization creates opportunities for teams
I will not lead a rigid life but follow ancient poets
Always linger on Zen wisdom my life quiet

八十壽祝賀

人間最重晚晴天
八十看成十八年
身健未愁雙鬢白
術高應得萬方傳
三春詩思能無夢
四化征途自有緣
我不長齋學蘇晉
從來就是愛逃禪

Remembering My Wife

I look for paradise blocked by blue seas under a green sky
In grief I find no way to Yellow Spring to bare my mind
East and west we had together weathered millions of strives
In hardship or happiness we kept together for sixty years
Forever I will remember your labour bringing up our children
And dare not forget the many tasty meals you offer at the table
Why am I left to be old alone I sigh
Only to keep up with teaching as days roll by

悼亡妻

望隔仙台碧海天
悲懷無計寄黃泉
東西曾共萬千里
苦樂相依六十年
永記辛勞培子女
敢忘賢惠佐鑽研
嗟余垂老何為者
兀自棲棲戀教鞭

Remembering Old Chums Back Home (I)

懷故鄉諸老友
（一）

Chums like colourful clouds disperse easily

Tasteless like plain water it is difficult to forget

I learned with grief many of you suffered inhuman threats

Now rectified I regret we are still wide spread

羣似彩雲原易散

淡如白水卻難忘

不堪閱盡風霜後

猶自逢春各一方

(II)

I embark on my life path not for money or fame
My heart with you my friends and home-soil remains
People say a floating cloud enjoys staying up the hills
My heart flies over the hills homeward still

（二）

不緣名利動征途
卻為友朋戀故磯
漫說浮雲出山久
鄉心依舊繞山飛

To the Summit of Mountain Heng (1961)

To the south side of this famous mount here I arrive
On the summit I dare to pick a star raising hands high
Beneath my eyes the blue River Xiang swiftly flows
To the depths of white clouds mountain ranges follow
For the red sun in a glorious sky I loudly sing
His mightiness shown his sword in swing
Fear not the roaring waves in the two oceans wide
To battle the whales on winds I ride

登衡山祝融峯（1961）

名山南峙此登臨
絕頂融峯敢摘星
眼底奔流湘水碧
巒巔追逐白雲深
我歌紅日經天麗
誰遣豪情仗劍行
莫道兩洋波浪闊
乘風飛去搏長鯨

East Wind (1967)

The east winds keep the blue Xiang River warm
They say fragrance urges the Wu Stream on
How I pine for my native home in autumn hue
Hills of maples their colours beacon frosts to yield

東風（1967）

東風吹暖碧瀟湘
聞道浯溪水亦香
最憶故園秋色裏
滿山楓葉艷驚霜

To My Wife from Prison (1969)

To return to battleground I am unable
Indebted I am to your love tall as clouds float
Grey hairs hurry the passing of years with no concession
Falsely indicted my life will continue to face oppression
A sick horse knows justice will not come even with calls
Withered palms are surely afraid to face biting frosts
Gone are past deeds forgotten like smoke in wind
My heart magnanimous my sky wide open

贈曾志（1969）

重上戰場我亦難
感君情厚逼雲端
無情白髮催寒暑
蒙垢餘生抑苦酸
病馬也知嘶櫪晚
枯葵更覺怯霜殘
如煙往事俱忘卻
心底無私天地寬

No Title

Separated by one cell we are blocked ten thousand fold
By lamplight I recall how we care for a common goal
Mornings up the mountain and moons by the Yan'an River
Could it be only a dream our coming together remembered

無題

一室相離阻萬重
遙憐燈下憶初衷
井崗曉日延河月
莫歎相逢是夢中

A Dream Remembered (1966)

My dream soars before dawn in winds and rains
The twilight world is hazy veiled by dews in swing
Words on surface say there is no tear in the country
Writing my thoughts on paper I cannot depart from reality
Noble friendship helps to defray extending disputes
Bloodshed coagulates the writing of poems old and new
I search the sky in silence for a promising road
The glares of dawn illuminate a world of hope

憶夢（1966）

五更風雨夢如飛
煙水蒼茫夜色微
話到海山無聲淚
寫來筆墨不沾衣
高情消盡千秋怨
碧血凝成萬古詩
默向長天尋新路
霞光芳霧映春暉

Tune: Charm of a Maiden Dancer–Remembering Jiao Yulu (1990)

Your soul in ten thousand li divagates

Its return I pray

To this our hills rills and land

Who among our people loves not a good public servant

See the huge Jiao Tongs your rainy tears have grown

On this sand dune you strived alone

On this sand dune your life doomed

Bound in life and death with people young and old

Through eve snows and twilight frosts

Your heroic spirit remains insistent

The moon shines bright today as yore

I pine for you in nights all

Our one-mindedness continuous in flow

Our road slow and far we together travel

Empty sleeves in clear winds to and fro

For just a singular civil post

To benefit communities in a territory

Happy you are in accomplishing a lifelong wish

Green my trivial dribbles

To fervent a thousand plains in pristine rambles

念奴嬌·追思焦裕祿（1990）

魂飛萬里
盼歸來
此山此水此地
百姓誰不愛好官
把淚焦桐成雨
生也沙丘
死也沙丘
父老生死繫
暮雪朝霜
毋改英雄意氣
依然月明如昔
思君夜夜
肝膽長如洗
路漫漫其修遠矣
兩袖清風來去
為官一任
造福一方
遂了平生意
綠我涓滴
會它千頃澄碧

中英對照近代中國風雲人物詩詞

POEMS OF SHAKERS OF MODERN CHINA –
ENGLISH TRANSLATION

附錄

毛澤東詩詞英譯隨想

毛澤東生前是國際風雲人物，1976 年逝世以後，更引起世人的評論和評價，包括對他的詩詞。

在近四十年間，中國人深切地認識了他的功過，並以寬容的心態讓人的作為跟隨時間長河流逝，積極建設現實，築夢未來。

詩傳情意

中國人在幾萬年的歷史文明建構中，創造出了十分美麗傳意傳情的文字，同時亦酷愛表達心聲，用詩詞唱出心靈深處的情感、理想和願望。中華民族各民族的詩作，在數量、意蘊和審美各方面，都高踞世界文學之顛。

有見及此，我們每人今天看着飛躍中的中國如何引起世界各地人們的興趣，在喜悅中不免反問自己，"我可否盡一己綿力，向世界介紹中國文化和詩詞？"。

政治和經濟問題十分龐大複雜，瞬息萬變，不是任何個人有能力沾手的。文化和藝術卻是恆定長久的東西，是知識份子可以提供貢獻的領域，尤其在促進溝通方面，詩詞翻譯至為重要。

溝通和了解

二十一世紀將誕前夕，國際學者發動多方面的研究，協力為新千禧時代提供指示，好讓人類和衷共濟，放棄二十世紀的仇視和殺戮，共創一個和諧共樂的未來。當時新成立的"科學探究學會"（Society for Scientific Exploration, SSE）專門研究宇宙間"反常和難以解釋的事情"，包括"人心"。

1988 年，我在普林斯頓大學高級研究學院（Institute for Advanced Study）訪問，向院長沃爾夫（Harry Woolf）請教他對人類未來的見解。他原是科學歷史專家，卻以教育學為研究重點，所以我們有過多方面的研究合作。他預言："教育必須幫助學生認識並獲得自尊，因為心智和意願將影響物質與社會和諧發展，消除仇恨、恐懼以及權力控制。"

1995 年，普林斯頓的科學家宣佈他們的實驗結果，證實："思想足以變更物質的隨機過程，把它變為可以預設完成的結果。"就是說，人的心智可以超越並改變事物的隨機性（randomness），主導"變動"（change）。

然而，人所主導的改變仍然難以預測。例如，我們於年尾看世界，誰能於年初預見，人們今天最關心和期待的，竟是"乾淨食物"？人類銳意創造愈來愈先進的資訊科技，卻遺忘了自己的吃喝需要。

ISS 於 1982 年成立，由全球 45 個國家 800 位科學家共同參與，研究有關人物的“不平常及未得解釋的各種現象”（unusual and unexplained phenomena）。大家得到一個共識，就是人類必須加強溝通和了解（mutual communication and understanding）。

毛澤東詩詞現象

說過這些話，我們可以回顧“毛詩現象”了，一個至今未解釋得清楚的“盛事”。它聯結着歷史、人文、文藝、個人心理、認識和國際溝通。

我在此呈現的 36 首英譯毛澤東詩詞，是他最重要的作品，包括他 1909 年的初作，和 1975 年的最後作品。

一個人六十六年的人生和寫作歷程，變動甚大，不論在公在私，經歷都是天翻地覆的時空及人事變動。

正是這樣，我們可以越過“隨機發生”的人身以外的大小事情，專注毛澤東詩人的情感（feelings），包括他的心智、慾望、抱負、情愛、關愛、矛盾、平靜、不安和懊悔（intelligence, desire, will, love and affection, caring, conflict and contradiction, peace, unrest, remorse）。

詩人是人，譯者亦是人，兩者都各有獨特的經驗、認知和情感，潛伏在他們的文化和文字素養裏面。假如兩者的這些屬性相若，翻譯的結果可以比較實在。相反，假如兩者不甚相干，結果可能演成生硬甚至失真的結果，不但不能促進溝通和了解，而且造成誤解。

稍為舉些例子。在美國一所著名大學裏面，有一位資深教授把最受人著稱的《雪》的翻譯如下：

北國風光 — 'Tis the wind and the light of the northern landscape that caught my feeling.
千里冰封 — The field is frozen in ice extending several hundreds of miles.
萬里雪飄 — And above ten thousand of miles the dazzling snow is flying.

同一首詞裏面的一句"風流人物"，被譯為 wind-flowing men，叫人看了莫明其妙。

這個譯本被選入大學課本，幫助莘莘學子欣賞毛詩詞的"美"和"雄偉"。但是，我真的很難想像怎樣可以促進溝通和瞭解。

在神州大地，毛詩的英譯亦不順暢，原因不在缺乏人才，而在驟然出現的政治衝擊。好像官方譯本只有一本，由幾位著名翻譯家主筆。他們在身處"反林反孔"的年代，對於怎樣翻譯毛主席的"子在川上曰……"，幾經集體思量都難以下筆。試問，又怎能把偉大詩人的名句傳達給外國朋友欣賞？

譯詩隨想

在翻譯這 36 首詩的過程中，我首先着重瞭解每首詩的歷史背景、時、空、人怎樣塑造毛澤東的心緒和心聲。

我的翻譯力求傳達原詩的意蘊和文字美。同時，我又稟承中國古詩體的特點，不加標點，旨在給讀詩人留下句與句之間的空間，讓他們自由"尋味"，或者填上個人的意義或馳想，使詩的翅膀騰飛邁遠。

毛詩充滿這樣的自由空間。試讀《重陽》：

　　　　人生易老天難老

　　　　歲歲重陽

　　　　今又重陽

　　　　戰地黃花份外香

首句比較人與天的暫在與恆久，即時跳入人間處理生死的節日。第四句提醒我們對革命犧牲者的敬意。毛澤東在四句簡潔的詩句中，寫下了宇宙人間的時、空和偉大事業。

我看毛澤東的情感，似乎他很少提及自己的父母。他熟讀古書，應該知道忠孝是做人之本，難道信奉了洋人的"馬列主義"，就可以放下中華文化中最重要的

"孝道"？

他長期與許多一同出生入死的"同志"赴湯蹈火，晚年
卻為了一己的執着，遺棄"忠道"，用殘酷的手段對待
他們。他的行為充滿矛盾。這些矛盾很容易見於他的
詩詞之中。這裏略舉數例說明。

- 彭德懷是毛的長期戰友和同鄉。他批評毛的大躍進
  政策陷全國農民於說謊和飢餓之中，被毛下放回
  鄉，加上多重打壓。1935 年，毛詩《給彭德懷同志》
  中說："誰敢橫刀立馬，唯我彭大將軍"，寫下
  多麼豪氣的讚賞。
- 在廬山會議之後，毛喜歡離開北京外居，借說首
  都空氣不好。在 1964 年發動文革前所寫的《有所
  思》，他明說"正是神都有事時"，然後在末句寫
  "故國人民有所思"，都是言為心聲的詩句。

1974 年，周恩來病危，受着四人幫的重重打擊，不能
控制大局。他勉強接待了到訪的加拿大總理杜魯多，
陪他遊覽"龍門"以後，坐上專機去長沙會見毛主席，
兩人談了半天。毛明知自己犯了大錯，讓妻子用愚蠢
和私心統管了神州大地，卻又不甘心讓它無辜地沉
淪。最後，在無奈中，他接受了周總理的建議，讓惟
一有才能掌理國家大事的鄧小平復出，扭轉神州面臨
的厄運。

在這種複雜的情感之下，毛寫成《贈周恩來》一詩，把

深藏心底的情懷盡訴於文字，同時總結自己的人生。
詞的下闋説：

> 業未就
> 身軀倦
> 鬢已秋
> 你我之輩
> 忍將夙願
> 付與東流

中國人今天可以回答"偉大舵手"，請他放心，中國已
經成為全球友好國家的羨慕和學習、西方國家所妒忌
的大國，而人民亦真正地當家作主，不受西洋意態的
綑綁。

毛詩的審美

話説回來，毛澤東的詩詞有很高的藝術價值。他的創
作不比李白所自稱的"攬彼造化力，持為我神通"。
然而，我們讀他的《長沙》，誰能不如身處大自然的勝
境，感到激動？試誦：

> 獨立寒秋　湘江北去　橘子洲頭
> 看萬山紅遍　層林盡染
> 漫江碧透　百舸爭流

他寫《長征》戰士們的革命豪情，行雲流水的文字，簡

潔平淡地刻劃出實情：

> 紅軍不怕遠征難
> 萬水千山只等閒

毛澤東善用隱喻，同時亦常用刻劃時空的尺寸，如千萬、億萬、萬般和蒼蠅等，要譯成英文又不倚賴註解，真不容易。他問："曾記否，到中流擊水，浪過飛舟"，喻意清晰，都只合"知心人"聽，而且留着無限的釋意可能。例如，"何者為浪？又何是飛舟？"，都有多種看法。

他説一句"不到長城非好漢"，只有去過長城兩端的人明白，那條從月亮下可看見的猛龍，從漠漠的關外伸延到東海，歷來雋明中華民族的真實情懷；我們只知防守，不事攻擊或侵犯他人。稍有頭腦的外國人都可以並應該放下"黃禍"的歪曲思想。甚麼叫好漢呢，我譯之為 a man tall，説明他高瞻遠矚，不計較眼前小事的得失，想是毛主席的原意。

1927 年的《菩薩蠻‧黃鶴樓》和 1956 年的《蝶戀花‧答李淑一》，都是上乘之作，寫下純靜平淡的"心"，而且想像騰飛，情深細膩，唐宋各家亦沒有幾人可以寫出這樣的純真美意：

> 我失驕楊君失柳
> 楊柳輕揚直上重霄九

問訊吳剛何所有
吳剛捧出桂花酒

在這 36 首詩詞之中，我欣賞至深的是詩人的純情之作，如《憶秦娥・婁山關》、《長沙》、《崑崙》、《重陽》、《答友人》、《卜算子・詠梅》、《重上井崗山》⋯⋯

結束本文之前，我必須再次說明。這些文字只記下讀詩和譯詩的隨想，不是有系統和精密心思的評論。我寄望文章和英譯可以幫助嚴肅的讀者深層了解和欣賞詩人毛澤東和他的佳作，止於此。

數學詩詞人生的對話

蘇步青是二十世紀的大數學家,專門研究微分幾何。在日本留學時期,他發現四次(三階)代數錐面,被稱為"蘇錐面",影響深遠。

他於 1902 年生於浙江省平陽縣的一個農村,家貧,於放牛時站在私塾窗前聽書,很快便背誦《三字經》和《百家姓》。九歲那年,他父親竭盡全力送他上學以後,每一階段都得到恩師幫忙。1919 年,他中學畢業,獲校長出資送他往日本留學。他用了三個月的時間掌握好日文,考入大學。這一份語文的天賦才能,讓他日後精通八種外文。

1924 年,他考入東北帝國大學的數學研究院,排名第一。他於七年後完成博士學位,當時已發表了 41 篇數學論文,成為他畢生發表 156 篇論文的"初試啼聲"。在中國,他是中國近代代數的奠基宗師,是學生喜稱的"幾何爺爺"。

在東北帝國大學讀書期間,他恩師的女兒米子看上了他,兩人於 1928 年結婚。她於 1933 年隨夫君返回中國,以後在中日戰爭的困難歲月中養育了八名子女,再經過文化大革命紅衛兵的侮辱和折磨,堅持本份。米子於 1986 年逝世,留下蘇步青獨居至 2003 年,終年 101 歲。

在大學裏，不到二十歲的蘇步青承接德國數學家克萊因（Felix Klein）提出的命題：每一種幾何面都聯繫一種變換羣。他心中想起童年放牛的時光，自己騎在吃飽了而變得弧形的牛背上，悠悠行着歸家，所見的盡是不同斜度的圓形變體，很是美麗。他於是進入斜變體變換本質的空間，畢生追求計算程式，發表他的創見。

1933 年，蘇步青從日本回到中國家鄉的浙江大學教學，回應好友陳建功的邀請。日本於 1937 年侵華，浙大遷去後方的貴州，他一家孩子眾多，過着窮苦和備受他人是非的生活。1945 年，他去台灣任教，兩年後歸國。1952 年，迎着新中國院校調整，他被分派到上海的復旦大學，於 1956 年升為副校長，於 1983 年任名譽校長。由他在東北帝國大學任代課講師（1927 年）到 1997 年他結束講課為止，他整整當了 70 年老師。

1968 年夏，"工宣隊"進駐復旦大學，開始抄蘇步青教授的家，指他為"資產階級反動學術權威"，以及"當日本特務"等莫須有的罪名。在十年動亂中，他被下放到農村和船廠做苦工，受盡辱罵和身心折磨。1974 年回校以後，他開始研究用仿射不變量方法引入計算幾何學，供電子工業應用。在八十年代，他又開創"幾何拓撲"的研究。

我於 1974 年初夏第一次會見蘇步青教授，大家在復旦大學的接見廳交換完客套話後，我建議到校園走走。

那時候中國仍然乍暖還寒，他由劉大杰教授陪同，我身邊則是賴恬昌和高錕同事。校園空寂一片，我心知他受過的身心打擊，暗自慶喜他仍然腳步穩健，精神平和，默默走了一會便誠心道別。

1982 年，我幫助中國振興重點大學，申請世界銀行貸款，到復旦聯絡。此時大學已恢復生氣，大環境的氣氛也寬鬆得多。我有機會第二次會見蘇老。那時他已經八十歲，卻興致十足，十分健談。

我不懂數學，逗他閒談語文和詩詞，因為我讀過他早年寫的《夜飲子愷先生家》，覺得它風格清新，表意幽默，直入人心，即如豐子愷的漫畫一樣。

他告訴我他喜愛語文，尤其是漢語，因為每個字都含着形與聲，影射着變換無窮的美麗空間，他自己就是從文字的幻想中馳想幾何學的變換形態，又從語文與數學的幻想中寫詩的。

時光和世態都在悠悠路程中過去，轉眼三十年。我於自己八十生辰時想起往事，查看舊筆記，見到與蘇老會談後陸續積存起他的一些詩作。讀之感慨萬千，即時進行翻譯成英文，讓更多人分享其中的的真誠意遠。

這裏用中英文呈獻給讀者的十九首詩詞，寫照着一個赤誠、勤奮、容忍、愛人、忠於職守和熱愛鄉土國家的中國人，在一世紀中不怕貧窮、屈辱、困苦和瘋狂打擊，一直堅持己任，不懈創新，及孕育後輩的足跡。

他用淡墨敍述夫妻不渝的愛情，表現出的竟是多幅彩色繽紛又百年瑩光的畫面，他用"武林"比喻學術殿堂，寫的不單是莘莘學子怎樣受老師無微不至的教導，同事間的互相勉勵，更指明科學文藝的鑽研空間無限，意義長明。他把一肚子的熱情留着表述對鄉土和祖國的依戀情懷和敬愛，不論身處何地，都情心緊繫。對於他個人的國際聲譽，他沒有沾上點墨。對於受苦和辱折，他隻字不提。

蘇步青先生的"業餘詩詞鈔"收刊了六百首詩詞。他生長在中國經歷外犯內鬥的二十世紀整整一百年間，沉默地履行"君子自強不息，厚德載物"的民族精神。給我們留下光輝人格的榜樣。

晚年，他在《數與詩的交融》裏面給青年們講話。他說："深厚的文學、歷史基礎是輔助我登上數學殿堂的翅膀。文學、歷史知識幫我開拓思路⋯⋯我要向有志於學理工、自然科學的同學們説一句話：打好語文、歷史基礎，可以幫你們躍上更高的台階。"